The Cas

Missing
Money

A BINA GOLD *Mystery*

The Case of The
Missing
Money

Rivka Chaya Berman

AURA PRESS
88 Parkville Avenue / Brooklyn, NY 11230

The Case of the Missing Money

ISBN 0-911643-24-9

Ruth Zakutinsky, General Editor
Shirley Kaufman, Series Editor

Printed in the U.S.A.

Published by
AURA PRESS, INC.
88 Parkville Avenue
Brooklyn, New York 11230
(718) 435-9103

FOR NACHMAN

AND

MOM AND DAD

Chapter One

With a loud bang, the classroom door slammed open. Talking stopped. Everyone stared at the threatening figure slumped in the doorway, wearing a disheveled, creased, dirty trench coat, a large hood thrown over the head partially covering the face. As the person staggered towards the teacher's desk, mumbling aloud, the girls trembled with fear.

Suddenly, the 'bum' threw off the coat and everyone gasped... Mrs. Mitchkin! Their teacher was dressed in an impeccably tailored, corporate-style, navy blue suit.

"Good morning class," she smiled, draping the coat over the back of her chair. "I would like to hear your reactions to what just happened."

"I thought that you were a drunken bum," Goldie called out, "and then, all of a sudden, you turned into an elegant, well-bred lady."

"So?" Mrs. Mitchkin encouraged.

"So the bum I would be afraid of and try to avoid, but with the elegant woman, well, I would sure watch my grammar."

Everyone laughed.

"But what if I told you that the muttering woman was a genius figuring out a complex theory, while the other woman was a petty thief who stole the clothes she had on?"

"We couldn't have known that," Shira said.

The class was paying rapt attention to the discussion. Last year, when Mrs. Mitchkin began teaching at Miami High, her flowery, flair skirts, colorful, beaded necklaces, combined with her sing-song voice, were not at all what the girls were accustomed to. She was very different, too strange to be taken seriously. Behind her back, she had been called 'the Merry Munchkin', but Mrs. Mitchkin persevered. After a difficult first semester, she had caught their attention with her dramatic way of bringing facts and lessons to life. Her unique approach had earned her a most-favored ranking among the students.

"It's one of our frailties as human beings that what we see on the outside, we perceive as true for the inside." Mrs. Mitchkin paused for effect. "When I was in ninth grade, my grandmother passed away. I hadn't been very close with her and felt guilty for not having made an effort to know her better. She had left me a large ruby pendant and matching bracelet. Feeling a need to connect with her, I began wearing the jewelry to school every day."

The teacher walked in front of the desk, her dangling earrings swinging back and forth. "Well, girls, you should have heard the names I was called: 'snob', 'poor little rich girl', to name a few of the nicer ones. No one bothered to ask why I was wearing the rubies. They just assumed I was showing off. I was hurting inside but no one seemed to care."

Karen, sitting in the back row, knew the feeling all too well. Everyone seems to make fun of me too. No one ever cares about how I feel.

"When I first came to this school, I didn't know how to *daven*," Rachel confessed. "It was so embarrassing because everyone knew how to pray, when to bow and what steps to make. I was afraid to ask anyone what page we were on or anything, thinking that if they knew, they wouldn't like me. So I mumbled my way through, hoping no one would realize how ignorant I was."

My heart bleeds for you, Rachel, Karen thought sarcastically. Afraid you weren't pious enough...afraid of being an out-cast...but your little prayers were answered, weren't they? You made it into a circle of friends. But me? Nobody wants me.

Doodles, taking the shape of frowning faces, swirling teardrops and other dark gashes, filled the pages of Karen's notebook as she listened to the discussion.

"The expression 'don't judge a book by its cover' fits here, I believe. What does that mean to you?" Mrs. Mitchkin looked around the room.

Bina raised her hand. "Just because something is good on the outside, doesn't always mean it is good on the inside. My mother puts the most frosting on the danish that has the least filling."

"Good," Mrs. Mitchkin smiled. "And not surprisingly, the concept of looking beyond the exterior is nearly the same idea as being *dan l'kaf zechus*, judging every person meritoriously. We must not only look inside a person, but we must assume that one's actions and motivations are honorable too. Unlike a cover," she held up the rumpled raincoat, "which can conceal the positive or negative aspects of a book, we, as Jews, are expected to look deeper to find the good within."

Karen's hand shot up. Maybe now her classmates could understand her pain.

Mrs. Mitchkin was happy to see her most unresponsive student participate.

"Yes, Karen?"

Karen froze. Unfriendly eyes stared at her. She fingered her doodle sheet that was nearly filled with black sketches. Lowering her eyes, she mumbled, "Nothing. I have nothing to say."

Mrs. Mitchkin's eyes lingered on her for a moment. "Okay. Anyone else?"

"Once I was shopping for a wallet in Leather Express," Goldie said. "When I tried to see if it would fit inside my handbag, the owner accused me of attempting to steal that ugly wallet. I ran out of there so fast. Now when I go to the mall, I make sure to avoid that whole section."

Karen's self-control went up in smoke. She bolted to her feet.

"Oh, you have no idea what it's like to really be judged unfairly," her shrill voice rang out. "To have people look at you like you don't deserve to share the very air they breathe. And worse, to have them totally ignore you. I'll bet that the second Mrs. Mitchkin walks out of this room, every one of you will forget everything she has just taught. Not judging a book by its cover, hah! That's all anybody ever pays attention to around here, the cover, and if it's not pretty they just walk right on by."

When Karen finished, she realized she was pointing a finger accusingly at Goldie.

Her arm dropped to her side and she collapsed into her seat. She wanted to faint or cry or run away, but she just sat there wishing she could miraculously disappear.

No one moved. No one spoke.

"Changing the way we view others is not something that can be done in one hour," Mrs. Mitchkin said softly, breaking the silence that followed Karen's outburst. "It will take a lot of effort. It takes sincere contemplation to see what and how we should improve and then hard work to bring about the change." As the bell rang, Mrs. Mitchkin concluded, "Remember, don't just think about what we said, act on it!"

Following Mrs. Mitchkin's exit, the walls of Miami Yeshiva High School's twelfth grade classroom resounded with high-pitched voices as the girls emphasized their viewpoints with fervor. Everyone had an opinion. Not many were shocked that although the lesson had focused on being non-judgmental, their comments ended up criticizing Karen.

Now I have really done it, Karen despaired, hearing snatches of the conversations around her. Why couldn't I have just kept quiet? Her nose began to prickle and her throat felt stuffy from unshed tears. She sat still, trying to think of something pleasant...her adorable little sister, Debbie. It didn't work. She felt her eyes melting.

"Want a tissue?" Bina offered, standing by Karen's desk.

"Thanks," she mumbled, taking it without looking up. She blew her nose.

Suddenly, she stood up, gathered her books, drew her cardigan around her shoulders and started walking to the door.

"Where are you going?" Bina followed.

"Go away," Karen snapped, walking faster. "I'm going home."

Bina rushed to keep up with her. "Hey, Karen, wait up!"

"What do you want?" she snarled.

"I just want to make sure you're okay."

Karen stopped and glared at her. "Well, I'm walking, breathing and talking. Now, Dr. Bina, are you satisfied that I'm okay or do you want me to take a throat culture?"

Bina bit the inside of her bottom lip.

Sometimes Karen could be so obnoxious.

"Karen, if you want to talk or anything, I..."

"No. I'm fine. Just leave me alone!"

Bina watched Karen storm out the front door, then turned and went back to class.

Chapter Two

As Bina re-entered the classroom, a rollicking cheer erupted.

"What's going on?" she asked Shira, slipping into her seat.

"Oh, you won't believe the good news. It's just too unbelievable."

"Tell me! Tell me!" She grabbed her friend's arm.

"Nope," Shira teased, with a wouldn't-you-like-to-know smirk.

"C'mon Shira. Do I have to beg?"

"Nah, I give in. Mrs. Schaeffer has just announced that we received an invitation to attend the Bais Yaakov Convention in New York."

"No way. You're kidding!"

"Nope." Shira's smirk turned into a full-fledged, ear-to-ear grin.

"That's amazing! When is it? Who will be going with us?"

"Sh. Mrs. Schaeffer is starting to speak."

Bina's mind traveled to New York. The skyscrapers, shopping in Boro Park and Manhattan, meeting all those new girls...it was going to be wonderful.

The annual Bais Yaakov Convention attracted religious girls from around the world. It was a week scheduled with activities, lectures and workshops. With the exception of a select number of schools, invitations were extended to Bais Yaakov sister schools exclusively. For Miami High to gain acceptance into this group meant that they were now known as a school with high standards of Torah observance and religious philosophy, on par with the venerable Bais Yaakov high schools.

As Bina's thoughts floated back to the classroom, she heard Mrs. Schaeffer say, "Each one of you must attend. The only way we can get a cheaper airfare is if we buy a certain amount of tickets." A rippling murmur went through the room. "Now, to eliminate hotel costs, we will be staying with families in Boro Park, the heart of New York's Jewish community, but we will have meals together in the Bais Yaakov dining room." She leafed through the papers in her hand. "The traveling expenses, the cost of meals and convention fee will come to three hundred and fifty dollars per person..."

Moans and groans drowned out the rest of Mrs. Schaeffer's sentence. Bina looked at her classmates, watching their reactions.

Throughout elementary school, the class had been separated into three distinct groups: the Brownies, the Goods and the Nursery group. Each group had teased and tormented the other. Upon entering high school, the inter-clique bickering had subsided. Now they co-existed in a tentative peace, but basically did not associate much with each other except when common goals arose, like pushing off a test date or raising money for the school library.

Would any ill-feelings surface before the trip that might cause a major rift among the groups? Bina wondered. Would everyone be as excited about going as she was? And could each girl raise the large amount of money needed to attend the conference? Bina fervently hoped that the prospect of attending the Bais Yaakov convention in New York would whet each one's appetite enough to overcome any difficulties.

Mrs. Schaeffer took Bina and Shira aside.

"This invitation is an honor for our school and it is important for us to be there. Try to convince everyone of this. It might be hard for some to raise such a large sum of money. Discuss it with everyone and see if there will be any major problems." Mrs. Schaeffer tucked the folder with her papers under her arm. "If money is a problem, you might want to think about having a fundraiser to lower each girl's cost."

"Okay," the girls said in unison. As president and treasurer respectively, Shira and Bina were expected to take the lead in class situations.

Mrs. Schaeffer nodded and left the room.

"Maybe we should talk to each group separately," Bina said thoughtfully when the lunch hour began. "That way we can tailor our remarks to their individual characteristics."

"Okay, let's go to the Brownies first." Shira linked her arm through Bina's and they headed outdoors.

The school 'backyard' was only a shared parking area, spanning the entire mall. All along the back fence were thick, green bushes, a couple of palm trees and, directly behind the school, one patch of grass and weeds. Under the glaring midday sun, the Brownies sat in a circle on that lone plot of green. Their group of five congregated there for lunch every sunny day, talking and tanning their way to a perfect golden brown. The query 'Did I get any color yet?' punctuated their conversations and was the impetus for their being dubbed the Brownies.

Classifying groups of classmates bothered Bina. She felt it eradicated the possibility of any one girl moving beyond her group. However, there was no denying that the Brownies had similar tastes (high fashion and low fat), opinions (never act undignified or overly interested) and customs (pizza at least once a week). Whenever Bina spoke to one of them, she always had the feeling that she was being judged for her ability to coordinate her outfit.

Shira began by addressing the Brownies' leader.

"Hi, Goldie. Isn't this great? I'm just dying to go on this awesome New York City trip."

"Really?"

"Like we get to go to the Big Apple for one whole week," Shira cooed, "and hang out with other Bais Yaakov girls." She was relying heavily on the lingo, but it seemed to engage the Brownies' attention...somewhat. "We'll be staying in Boro Park where there are exclusive shops galore."

Bina watched Goldie closely. A small smile appeared briefly and then was gone. Her reaction seemed positive but with a Brownie, one never knew for sure.

"Sounds interesting, but Mrs. Schaeffer said we aren't going to be staying in a hotel. I just can't see spending three hundred and fifty dollars to be stuck in someone's grimy basement."

Shira shot Bina a desperate look.

"You know," Bina said quickly, "let's not talk accommodations until we're sure everyone is planning to go. So, like, do you think you," Bina glanced at the others, "can manage to come up with three hundred and fifty bucks?"

"That is not the problem," Goldie said abruptly and turned her back on them. They got the message loud and clear. The conversation was over.

Shira and Bina sauntered away.

"We almost got through to them, didn't we?" Shira asked hopefully.

"Don't know. I'm sure they'll at least consider it," she answered. "Goldie did seem to like the idea of shopping in Boro Park and no one flinched at the amount of money."

They looked back and saw the Brownies resume their modest tanning positions: sleeves rolled to the elbow, shining faces turned to the sky.

"Now onto the Goods," Bina said, hoping they would do better with the others. They headed for the lunchroom.

The Goods always sat in the first row of

every class listening attentively to every lecture no matter how dull. When a teacher announced a term project that was due in three months, the Goods began working on it that same night. Their work was regularly handed in early. Their textbooks were always neatly covered. Their pencils were perpetually pointy. The Goods were certain to remind a teacher if she forgot to assign homework. They were the first to volunteer for time-consuming projects like visiting hospitals or packing donated clothing for the needy in Israel.

"Aren't you excited about the trip to New York?" Bina exclaimed, approaching their lunchroom table. "Outstanding Torah scholars from around the country will be speaking. I can't wait to hear them."

"Likewise, but the cost bothers me," Rena said. "Perhaps we should use the money to help those who are truly in need."

Bina thought quickly. "Maybe we should have a fundraiser. Some of the money could go to reduce everyone's cost and the rest could be donated to a worthwhile cause."

"Now that's an interesting idea," Rena said and returned to eating her lunch.

The last group was the Nursery girls who, except for Bina, had been together since pre-school. When Bina had skipped fourth grade and landed in their class, Tammy, a Nursery girl who recently moved to Israel, befriended her and before long, they all became close friends. Now it seemed as if they had known each other forever.

These girls were the ones Bina felt most comfortable with. No matter how preposterous her suggestions, the Nursery girls were sure to hear her out. With them, she could be herself. They were all roaring to take New York City by storm.

Bina and Shira gulped down their lunch and, as usual, headed off to the bakery next door to buy a gooey caramel-pecan roll for dessert.

Miami High's temporary 'campus' consisted of two store-sized spaces with additional rooms upstairs, rented in a well-kept mall. The plus side to this location was that there was a large parking lot in the back which the school shared with the other stores, not to mention the incredible convenience of having a bakery, a hair salon, a stationery store and a bank close by.

On the down side, the shopkeepers had not been thrilled about having the school there. Apparently, they had worried that the students would be rowdy and drive away their clientele.

Bina remembered the persuasions and concessions that her father, the principal of a local boys' yeshiva, and other community members had to offer in order to gain permission to establish the school there. Deals had been made.

As a result, the school was always doing favors for the neighboring stores. When the beauticians, two stores down, went on vacation, some of the girls had been enlisted to water their plants and collect their mail. When the stationery store's fax machine broke down, Miami High had volunteered to receive faxes for them, until theirs could be fixed.

The bakery, however, was the one who

used their services to the utmost. Nearly every day, Jacko Chimley, owner of Chimley's Kosher Chewies, slinked over to the office to use their telephone, borrow paper or mooch a few stamps. And since Chimley was not Jewish, he needed someone Jewish to light the fires in his ovens everyday so his baked goods would be permissible according to Jewish law. He used Miami High teachers to fill that need.

"You know, Shira, I just don't get it," Bina said, as they entered Chimley's dimly-lit store, taking a number and waiting in line. "Look how busy this place is. Chimley has to be raking in tons of money and he still uses our phone and everything. It's not like he can't afford his own supplies."

"You're right. Maybe he just likes hanging out with Mrs. Palanchio."

Bina thought of the school's rancorous secretary and laughed. "I don't think so."

"Which lovely girl has number seventeen?" Jacko Chimley called out from behind the cream puffs.

"Oh, we do." Bina and Shira stepped up to the counter.

Chimley was chomping on his ever-present toothpick. The soggy toothpick, combined with the grimy jacket he wore, was enough to make you lose your appetite. Well, almost.

"Doughnut you know what you want?" Chimley ran his fingers through his greasy hair and grinned, enjoying his weak pun. "If you need help making up your mind, just cream...I mean, scream for me."

Bina sighed with exasperation. She wished she could avoid his sick humor.

"Just a caramel-pecan roll, please."

He grabbed an oozingly luscious roll with a piece of wax paper and handed it to her. After paying, Bina split it with Shira and they headed back to school.

"Facing that slimy man is worth it for one of these," Shira purred, swallowing her first bite.

"Yum, it is so delicious," Bina agreed. "I would love to try one of those chocolate pastries. Don't the pictures of the choco-mulas on the wall-poster look luscious? But at $16.50 a piece, it's just too expensive."

"The sign says, 'By Special Order Only'.

I wonder who orders such expensive items."

Before Bina could respond, the bell rang, signalling the end of the lunch hour.

Bina spent the rest of the day trying to figure out how to convince her parents to pay for the trip. She had used all of her savings this past Chanukah to go to Israel. Since then, she had not earned anywhere near the amount needed.

Chapter Three

The Brownies had been the first ones to bring in their funds. Ten days later, only a handful of girls had not yet paid for the trip.

As she did every day before the first class began, Bina sat at the teacher's desk collecting money. She felt very official doing the job she was elected to do as class treasurer.

Today, Rena was first. She handed Bina her permission slip and payment — a check and a neat pile of bills. Bina stashed it into the envelope.

"How are we doing?" Shira asked, stepping up to the desk.

"Not bad. Almost everyone has brought in their money. But could you please step aside? Others are waiting to pay."

Bina's official attitude amused Shira. She followed orders and retreated to her own desk.

Karen did not wait in the line to give money to Bina. She attempted to look as nonchalant as possible, hoping that no one would notice that she had not brought in her share. Mrs. Schaeffer will just have to find someone else to take her place at the convention, Karen thought bitterly.

Bina went over her list. Everyone except Karen Richter had paid. She glanced at Karen, sitting alone as usual. Since coming to Miami High last year, Karen had never become friendly with anyone. Maybe she didn't want to go to the convention because she thought she would be all alone there. But, then again, maybe she just didn't have the money. Bina circled Karen's name. She would talk to Mrs. Schaeffer. Perhaps the principal could work something out if money was the problem.

She gathered her papers and walked to Shira's desk. "Looks like we did it."

"Really?" Shira jumped up and turned to her classmates. "This is incredible. When the trip was first announced, we weren't sure everyone could raise so much money. We were so sure it was going to be a slow uphill crawl." She smiled broadly. "But we did it. You know what this means, don't you? It means we are definitely, for sure, going to the great state of..." she paused.

"New York," everyone shouted. Cheers, applause and a general ecstatic feeling swirled about the room.

"The next step," Bina said, as the noise subsided, "is to go to the bank and cash all of this." She waved the envelope. "Then, I'll put all the money in Mrs. Palanchio's desk until the tickets can be purchased."

As another roar rocked the seniors' classroom, Karen sank deeper into her seat, trying to avoid eye contact with her jubilant classmates. Even in the euphoria, Bina noticed Karen's discomfort. She walked over to her just before the science teacher entered the classroom.

"Karen, I'm going to the bank now. Do you want to come with me?"

Karen was about to rebuff Bina and tell her once and for all that Karen Richter did not need Bina Gold's charity, but then she reconsidered. She hadn't done her science homework the night before.

"Do you think Mrs. Schaeffer will let me go with you?"

"I'll just tell her that I need you as my bodyguard," Bina grinned.

After a quick stop in the principal's office for a note to show Mrs. Palanchio, whose sharp eyes guarded the front door, Bina and Karen were off.

The muggy Miami air, warm for November, closed around them as they made their way to Coastal Bank at the end of the mall. Bina tried to make conversation, hoping Karen would volunteer a reason for not bringing in her money.

"I am so excited about the convention. I can't wait to see New York. Have you ever been there?"

"No."

"I haven't either, but I hear that they have the best bagels. I'm a bagel fanatic." Getting no response, Bina kept up her chatter. At least they were not walking in awkward silence. "And I can't wait to see all those fancy stores in Boro Park."

Bina's mouth runs on like a river, Karen thought. Why can't we just walk in peace?

"Jean is my favorite teller at the bank." Bina said, as they entered the building. "She is so nice. I think she really likes our school or something, you know?"

Karen settled into a firm vinyl chair near the front door. Bina could visit her friend Jean all by herself. As Karen watched Bina's enthusiastic conversation with the teller, she knew she wasn't missed. No change there, she thought. No one ever misses me...except my family.

Bina returned, beaming with joy.

"Okay, I've got the cash. Let's go!"

As they walked back to school, it started to drizzle.

Karen said suddenly, "Bina, you go on without me, I'll, uh, see you later."

"Where are you going?"

"What's it your business?" Karen snapped.

"Just wondering."

"I have to stop at the bakery, okay? Don't worry, I'm not crossing the street so

I don't need you to hold my hand."

"Are you hungry? You can have some of my lunch if you want."

"No, thank you," she said curtly. "I just have to see my boss, so why don't you stop with the mothering, okay?"

"All right. I guess I'll see you later."

Bina knew that Karen worked for the strange man at the bakery. She saw Karen going to work there almost every day after school. The girls in the Nursery group thought that Chimley's odd ways were rubbing off on Karen, making her even more unpleasant lately.

"Young lady, did you take that envelope from the school's supplies?" demanded the ever-vigilant Mrs. Palanchio, as Bina entered the office. "I don't see your name on the request sheet."

"No. I brought it from home, Mrs. Palanchio."

Mrs. Palanchio took her role as secretary very seriously. She viewed herself as guardian of the school. In addition to her official duties, she had added some of her own: keeping the students from using the office phone and chastising teachers for wasteful usage of supplies and the copy machine.

She had become even more vigilant after a few computers disappeared from the building last year. The thieves were never caught. Although she was never a suspect, she thought, falsely, that people wondered if she was involved. Since then, Mrs. Palanchio had made it her business to be an outstanding employee. She arrived early every day and was always willing to work overtime.

"Mrs. Palanchio, all the money for our class trip to New York is in here." Bina held up the manila envelope. "I need to put it somewhere until we can go to the travel agency. I thought your desk would be a safe place."

Mrs. Palanchio's face brightened. "You may put the money in the bottom drawer. It will be safe there until you need it." She bent down and, using her conspicuous purple key, unlocked the drawer. "Do it quickly now. I have to go to a dress-fitting appointment shortly and I must straighten up the office first."

They were suddenly distracted by Jacko Chimley's noisy entrance.

"Hey, Mrs. Palamino, I mean Mrs. Palanchio," Chimley heehawed loudly as he stomped to the desk near the back wall. "You don't mind if I use the phone, right?"

He grabbed the telephone just as Mrs. Solomon, the *Shulchan Aruch* teacher, who taught Jewish laws and customs, was reaching for the receiver. She glared at Chimley, then strode to Mrs. Palanchio's desk, snatched up the second phone line and started dialing.

"Mrs. Solomon, I have informed you countless times that these telephones are for school use only," Mrs. Palanchio huffed. "And I really must have at least one line free at all times."

"This is important, Mrs. Palanchio. I'll only be a minute," the teacher answered. "Hi, David. I can't stay on the phone. I just wanted to tell you that the reservation is confirmed and you will be driving Bubby to the airport this evening." She paused for a moment, listening. "I put it on my credit card. I'll worry about how to pay for it later. After all, it's only once-in-a-lifetime that her sister in Israel will have a fiftieth wedding anniversary party."

The photocopier repair man, busy tinkering with the machine's smudgy innards, was muttering to himself. The metal paper tray fell to the floor making a loud, sharp noise which made everyone jump.

As Bina put the envelope with the money into the bottom drawer, she watched the commotion with amusement. Mrs. Palanchio looked harassed, trying to keep an eye on everyone.

Mrs. Schaeffer suddenly appeared at the door. "Mrs. Palanchio, please bring the first-aid kit, quickly. Shira's hurt," and she immediately disappeared.

Mrs. Palanchio snatched the kit off the shelf and lumbered out the door, grumbling, "Wouldn't you know something has to happen to make me late for my Theresa's first wedding dress fitting."

Bina rushed ahead of the complaining woman. Out of the corner of her eye, she noticed Karen enter the school and head for the office. She was surprised because she had thought Karen would cut school for the rest of the day.

Pushing her way through the crowd surrounding her friend, she asked wryly, "Any last words, Shira?"

"Bina, how can you joke at a time like this?"

"Sorry, buddy. What happened?"

Mrs. Palanchio arrived and handed the first-aid kit to Mrs. Schaeffer, who bandaged Shira's left pinky.

"Wouldn't you know it. The second I get my turn to dissect that little frog over there, I cut myself with the scalpel. You should have seen me. I was gushing!"

"Gross."

"Thanks for your support, Bina."

"Well, how about some good news? The money is in the office. Does that make you feel better, Madame Class President?"

"It sure does."

"Hey, maybe we can go to the travel agent with Mrs. Schaeffer during lunch." Bina looked at the principal, who was packing up the first-aid kit. "Is that all right, Mrs. Schaeffer?"

"Sure, that will be fine," she answered, looking around. "Did anyone see where Mrs. Palanchio went?"

No one had seen her leave.

Morning sessions passed. Teachers and students paraded according to schedule from classroom to classroom. Teachers lectured. Some girls paid attention. Some minds wandered. Bells rang. The drinking fountains quenched thirsts. Sinks clogged and overflowed in the bathrooms. The copy machine broke down again. It was lunch.

Shira was busy copying someone's lab notes. "I'll be finished shortly, Bina. Go get the money and I'll meet you in the lunchroom."

"Righto. Write neatly 'cause I'll need to copy those notes later," Bina said, as she hurried out of the room.

The office was empty for a change. Mrs. Palanchio's desk was a mess. She must have been really late for her appointment, Bina thought.

Bina tugged open the bottom drawer.

The envelope was not there. She stuck her hand under the papers in the drawer. She sifted through paper clips and rubber bands. No envelope. How could that be? She tried the other drawers. They were all locked. She scoured through the mess on top of the desk. She fell to her knees and looked under the desk. The money was gone!

Chapter Four

"We've been robbed!" Bina cried as she ran into the lunchroom. "The money's gone. I can't find it anywhere!"

Everyone began talking at once. The sun-loving Brownies, forced to eat inside because of the rain, joined the Goods and Nursery groups in angry protest.

"What?" "Oh no!" "What are we going to do?" "Fingerprints! Someone should dust for fingerprints!"

Hearing the commotion, Mrs. Schaeffer approached.

"Girls, girls, what is going on?"

Trembling, Bina told her.

"Are you sure you put the money in the bottom drawer?" Mrs. Schaeffer asked.

Bina nodded sadly. Robberies were

uncommon at Miami High.

"We should call the police," Chana demanded. "The perpetrator should be prosecuted to the full extent of the law." Chana's father was a lawyer.

"Girls, please calm down. I'm sure there is a perfectly logical explanation for this. I will speak with Mrs. Palanchio. Perhaps she put it somewhere else."

As soon as Mrs. Schaeffer left the lunchroom, everyone began venting their feelings. They were very upset.

"Do you know how many hours I had to baby-sit to raise that much money?" Leah asked no one in particular. "Fifty...no, way over fifty hours of running after little kids, and for nothing."

"I can't believe this. My parents are going to kill me. Do you know how much I pestered them for the money?" Chana wrung her hands. "I begged and pleaded and cried. I drove them absolutely crazy. They will never replace so much money."

Bina staggered to her lunch table and stood with her head lowered. Then she heard someone say, "Don't you think it's kind of odd that the money disappears right after it gets into the student council's hands?" She cringed, sat down and buried her head in her arms.

"Bina." Shira tapped her friend on the shoulder.

"What?" she answered without looking up.

"Are you okay?"

"Not really," Bina sniffed. "They are blaming me for losing the money."

Shira wanted to say something supportive to wash away her friend's hurt. She wanted to tell Bina that she was mistaken, that no one was accusing her, but it would not be true. So, she just stood there as silent testimony that no matter what, she would always be her friend.

"Maybe you put the money in one of Mrs. Palanchio's other drawers or something," Shira mumbled finally.

"No, I didn't. The money is gone."

Mrs. Schaeffer returned. "Bina, may I speak with you please?"

The investigation into the missing money had begun. A splotch of red appeared on

Bina's cheeks as she walked past her classmates and followed the principal to her office. She felt that those girls who were whispering and hinting that she was somehow guilty, would now speak with more authority. Bina's being summoned to the office would seem to confirm their suspicions.

"Tell me once again about the circumstances under which you left the money," Mrs. Schaeffer began as soon as they were seated.

Bina reviewed everything starting with her walk to the bank with Karen. When Bina mentioned Mrs. Palanchio's appointment with the dressmaker, Mrs. Schaeffer seemed surprised.

"She never told me about the dressmaker. She merely said that she had an appointment."

"Maybe she thought you wouldn't let her go if it wasn't a doctor's appointment."

"I don't think so. Mrs. Palanchio always tells me..." Mrs. Schaeffer's voice trailed off as she sat thinking. "Well, maybe Mrs. Palanchio put the envelope somewhere else." The bell rang. Lunch was over. "Thank you, Bina. You may go to class now."

Bina stepped out of the office and saw Shira leaning against the wall.

"You keeping guard or something?"

"I just wanted to see if Mrs. Schaeffer would eat you for lunch. Actually, I thought you might need someone to talk to."

"I do, but right now we have to go to class. Can you come to my house after school? We can talk better over cookies and ice-cream."

"It's a deal. Boy, do we have a lot to talk about. We will have to figure out a way to raise enough money so everyone can still go to New York."

Time could not pass quickly enough for Bina. She could not wait for the school day to end. As soon as the bell rang, she and Shira grabbed their books and practically ran all the way to Bina's house.

They burst through the front door and followed their noses to the kitchen where Mrs. Gold was rolling out some dough.

"Hi, Ma." Bina said sadly. "You won't

believe what happened today," and she told her mother about the missing money.

"That's terrible," Mrs. Gold commiserated. "Does anyone have any idea who could have taken it?"

"No, not yet. Shira and I are going to brainstorm to see if we can come up with a way to raise money for the trip. But we need some fuel for our brains." She walked to the oven and peeked inside. "Ooh, I think I found just the thing."

"Sorry to disappoint you, Bina, but those rugelach are for *Shabbos*. You can have the cookies I made yesterday."

"Okay. Thanks, Mom."

Arming themselves with spoons, bowls, a pint of vanilla-swirl ice-cream and cookies, they scampered off to Bina's room.

They passed under an arch into a long hall. On both sides were tall, crammed bookcases extending the full length of the walls. Many of the Hebrew volumes dealt with scholarly Jewish subjects; there was a set of the *Talmud* and row upon row of leather-bound commentaries. Other books were in the 'ology' category: biology, ecology and geology, reminders of Bina's parents' college years, and added recently, psychology textbooks. Bina's mother had returned to college to complete her Masters' degree in School Psychology.

Nearest to Bina's green and beige room was her own personal bookcase. It had an eclectic collection of mysteries, gourmet cookbooks and computer-programming manuals.

Shira sat down on the bed as Bina scooped ice-cream into each bowl.

"These cookies are delicious. Did you make them?" Shira licked the crumbs off her fingers.

"My mom did, using a recipe I cut out of a magazine."

Shira picked up the magazine lying on the night table. "Car magazines have baking recipes?" she asked incredulously, turning the pages.

"No," Bina giggled. "That's Yossi's."

"Wow, look at this car," Shira exclaimed.

"Isn't it something? It's a Porsche. Very expensive. My brother says it's his dream car." Bina took the magazine and flipped to another page. "But see this one? That's my dream car. It's a Lamborghini. It's four or five times more expensive than a Porsche." She handed it back to Shira. "I love reading about the latest cars. One day, when I'm old enough and rich enough to have my own, I'll know exactly which one to buy."

"Sounds like you already know," Shira said dryly, as she held up the picture of the Lamborghini.

They both burst out laughing.

"Okay, let's get down to business." Shira put aside the magazine. "We have to figure out a way to replace the lost money. I was thinking, how about a bake sale?"

"That's so unoriginal, Shira. Who hasn't done that over and over again?"

"Do you have any better ideas?" Shira was annoyed. "It's not like we have so much time to come up with something out of this world, you know."

Bina frowned. Shira was right.

"Okay. A bake sale could be a really good idea. Tried and true, as they say. We could even make a version of chocomulas. They won't taste as good as Chimley's but I'm sure people would buy them if they were a quarter of his price." She licked her spoon slowly. "And maybe we could add a little spice to it by auctioning off the goods, instead of just selling them."

"Hey, that's a great idea." Shira smiled. "I just heard about this major auction that raised thousands of dollars with just one bottle of vintage wine."

Bina sighed. "Let's hope we can raise half of the money we need. It still won't be enough."

"The only way to get enough would be to find the missing money," Shira lamented. "But, by now, whoever stole it is probably halfway to Europe or wherever people go after committing a robbery."

"Don't you think someone would have noticed if an underworld character had entered our school?"

"That's true." Shira crossed her legs and leaned back against the pillow. "It seems to me that it would have to be someone who knew where you put the money. What about that repairman? You said he was in the office at the time."

"I don't know. Why would he jeopardize his job at the school? He must make a mint from Miami High. He's always coming back to replace a part or to unjam a paper."

"Maybe the school owes him money."

Bina scoffed. "If we're going to consider everyone owed money by the school, the list will be very long. Everyone knows that Miami High is always struggling to just pay its teachers' salaries." Bina reached for another cookie. "But you gave me a good idea. Let's focus on who was in the office when I put the money there." Bina closed her eyes. "Mrs. Solomon was there."

"Mrs. Solomon?" Shira laughed. "Why would she take our money? She was one of the school's original teachers. That's impossible."

"She was on the phone, talking about how she sent some grandmother on a trip to Israel, even though she knew she couldn't really afford to pay for it."

"Very funny. Can you imagine that

someone who taught us about honesty and the importance of *hashovas aveida*, the laws of returning lost items, would do such a thing?" Shira stabbed at her ice-cream with the spoon, lowering her voice. "Some of the girls think that maybe Mrs. Palanchio did it."

"Yeah, right!" Bina snorted.

"I don't think we should rule anyone out. Right now, everyone should be considered a suspect. Let's make a pro and con list to weigh everyone's guilt or innocence. We'll start with Mrs. Palanchio."

"That's sounds like an idea Daniel would come up with, so clinical," Bina said playfully.

It was true, Bina thought. Her older brother, whom she adored, would have handled the matter in the same way. He had moved to Israel soon after his marriage. Too bad he was so far away, otherwise his cool, clear logic could have helped them come up with ideas.

"Okay." Bina pulled a notebook and pen out of her backpack. "One. Mrs. Palanchio knew exactly where the money was." She chewed on the pencil for a moment. "Two. She disappeared so quickly afterwards. When I came back to the office to get the money, she was gone."

"And nobody would think twice if they saw Mrs. Palanchio walking out of the office with an envelope," Shira added.

With a frown, Bina marked down those points on the con side of her chart.

"What about motive?" Shira said.

"Good point." Bina doodled on the corner of the paper. "You know, she mentioned her daughter's wedding. I remember when Daniel married Elisheva, the bills drove my parents crazy. I guess wedding costs could be a motivation for driving someone over the edge."

"Do you think those girls who suspect her are right?"

"We can't blame someone, who may not even be guilty, without any proof," Bina cautioned. "It's terrible to be falsely accused."

"Yeah, I guess you're right. And there's one major thing that's certainly in Mrs. Palanchio's favor. Her loyalty to the school."

"That's so true. She's been working at Miami High for years," Bina said. "If she had the urge to increase her salary by secretly taking school money, wouldn't she have done so years ago? She must have had debts in the past too. Every family has trouble making ends meet at one time or another. If she was honest all these years, it doesn't seem logical for her to change now."

"That was so moving, Bina," Shira cheered, wiping away an imaginary tear. "Mrs. Palanchio definitely deserves our trust. We cannot let her down."

"Yeah," Bina responded glumly.

They sat in silence considering the chart before them. The points for and against Mrs. Palanchio's innocence were neatly listed, but they were of no help at all.

Chapter Five

The next morning, Mrs. Palanchio's desk was vacant. A big bold sign was posted on the door:

DO NOT TOUCH ANYTHING ON MY DESK! ANYONE CAUGHT NEAR MY DESK WILL BE SEVERELY PUNISHED! CONSIDER YOURSELF WARNED!

MRS. PALANCHIO.

The teachers were relieved that the secretary was not there to bother them for congregating in the office. They made their photocopies in peace. The students were happy because no one stopped them at the door demanding a note. But, somehow, without Mrs. Palanchio's ever-vigilant hawk eyes surveying the early morning rush to class, the school day did not seem to start out quite right.

Goldie was waiting in the hall outside Mrs. Schaeffer's office. She had been sent to the principal's office for spraying some girls with a water gun; unfortunately one girl had ducked and the spray splashed a passing teacher instead.

Goldie buffed her nails against her blouse as she waited. She could hear Mrs. Palanchio's voice coming from inside and she leaned closer, but could only catch a word here and there. "...my desk...must have forgotten to...daughter's wedding ...money...I can't believe...didn't take..." Goldie thought her tone sounded very defensive.

Aha. Now Goldie knew why Mrs. Palanchio wasn't at her desk. She was evidently being confronted for stealing their money. Goldie decided that Mrs. Schaeffer could punish her later and hurried back to her classroom. Standing outside the door, peering through the window, she surreptitiously waved until she caught Leah's attention.

Leah excused herself from class and joined Goldie in the hall. "What's up?"

"Mrs. Schaeffer has found the thief," Goldie whispered breathlessly. "Mrs. Palanchio is in her office right now trying to weasel her way out of it. It seems Mrs. Palanchio took our money to pay for her daughter's wedding."

"Are you sure?"

"Of course I'm sure. I overheard Mrs. Palanchio say so myself."

Leah's eyes widened. "Wait until everyone hears about this!"

As word spread throughout the school of Mrs. Palanchio's suspect status, a few girls in the twelfth grade and some in the lower grades sought to catch a glimpse of the accused worker. A steady stream of curious students found excuses to be in the office, hoping to see some guilty behavior to bolster their claims.

"Can I have a paper clip?"

"Can you take my temperature?"

"My teacher sent me to get some chalk."

Each one walked away with an opinion which they eagerly shared with anyone willing to listen. The halls of Miami High reverberated with gossip.

"She was just sitting there without any change of expression. As if nothing had happened," a breathless Leah confided to Goldie.

"She's probably plotting a defense strategy. I can't believe Bina was so stupid as to actually leave the money with her," Goldie said saucily. "Didn't she know that a woman who throws temper tantrums over missing pencils would not be very reliable?"

"Excuse me," said Bina.

Goldie blushed. She had not known that Bina was within earshot.

"I thought that because Mrs. Palanchio is so particular, she would be extra vigilant and ensure that the money would be safe."

Estee joined in, "Yeah. How was Bina to know that she would do such a thing?"

"Estee!" Bina glared at her friend. "That's not what I meant at all. Until we know for sure, it's wrong to accuse anyone."

"Well, still..." Goldie paused. "Once we had a housekeeper who we suspected of taking our silverware. She also acted like she didn't know anything about it. My parents finally fired her, but until they did, I would leave the room whenever she entered. She gave me the creeps..."

"Goldie," Bina cut in, "It's not right to compare Mrs. Palanchio to your housekeeper. We should not find someone guilty before we have proof."

The Brownies, Goods and Nursery girls all crowded around, curious to hear what Bina and Goldie were talking about.

"I think Bina's right," Ilana, a Brownie, spoke up. "And maybe we should be considering other people."

"Like who?" Aviva challenged.

"Like someone who did not seem to want to go to the convention in the first place," Ilana said, nodding toward Karen Richter who was standing near a window.

The group gasped.

Realizing that she was the center of attention, Ilana preened. "When everyone was giving Bina the money, I happened to glance at Karen."

"Why would you do a dull thing like that?" Goldie cackled.

"Who knows," Ilana was not going to let Goldie steal the spotlight, "but I noticed that Karen did not look very happy. In fact she kept staring at the money."

Bina was about to cut in to denounce the accusations when Ariella, a Nursery girl, spoke up.

"You know, Karen is a little strange. I mean, remember when she first came to our school? Some of us tried to befriend her but she wouldn't respond. She acted so snobbish. And she never talks in class, except for that one time when she blew up in Mrs. Mitchkin's. She never comes to any student council parties. She's very aloof."

Ilana added her opinion: "She works at Chimley's, and although I love his pastries, that Jacko Chimley is a weirdo and maybe it rubs off on those who get too close to him. Sometimes she seems really spaced out."

"You know, you could be right," Ariella said.

The conversation was definitely

surprising. Not only were the Brownies and Nursery girls talking together, but they were actually agreeing on something.

Bina, however, was not impressed. True, her classmates were interacting amicably, for a change, but it was only to defame Mrs. Palanchio or accuse Karen Richter.

"I can't believe you guys," Bina stammered. "Are you so desperate to see your money back that you are willing to blame anyone? Have you no sense of decency? You..."

"I totally agree with Bina," Shira interrupted, putting her arm around Bina's shoulders. "Instead of pointing fingers, let's discuss how to raise some cash to replace the lost money."

Karen inched closer to hear what was going on.

Shira decided to seize this opportunity while everyone was together to promote the bake sale. "I think a bake sale is a good, fast way to generate money for the trip. And to make it interesting, perhaps we could auction the items instead of just selling them." Shira looked at each girl. "What do you think?"

"Yeah. Good idea," they all chorused.

"But time is of the essence. How about baking tomorrow evening? We can have the auction the next day. Who's available?"

Aside from Karen, everyone raised their hands.

"Good. I'll get Mrs. Schaeffer's permission to use the school's kitchen and the cooking class' baking supplies," Shira continued. "All you have to do is show up at seven. I expect to see everyone there with their best dessert recipes in hand."

With that, their Hebrew language teacher arrived and everyone followed her into the classroom.

"Thanks for saving me from going overboard, Shira," Bina whispered.

"No problem," Shira replied. "Don't let them get to you. They just babble."

The next day, Bina dashed home after the dismissal bell. There was only a few hours to eat dinner and do her homework before she had to be back at school for the baking night. She barely stopped to greet her mother, grabbing a handful of cookies and hurrying to her room to begin her assignments.

As the only girl in the family, Bina never had to share a room. While Princess Bina, as her brothers were wont to call her, had an elegant queen-sized bed, the boys, 23-year-old Daniel and 11-year-old Yossi, had had to cram into one room with bunk beds. Things were more comfortable for Yossi now that Daniel was out of the house.

After dinner, Bina flipped through her file of recipes. She was looking forward to the evening. She loved baking and experimenting with different ingredients and techniques and was very good at it.

The doorbell rang.

"Bina, someone's here to see you," Yossi called.

"Coming."

She smiled at the familiar-looking girl standing in the foyer. She could not recall who she was.

"Hi, please come in." She led the way into the living room. "May I get you something to drink?"

"Sure, water will be just fine," the tanned teenager said.

"Have a seat. I'll be back in a second."

Bina went into the kitchen. The face is definitely familiar, but who is she? It was embarrassing not to know someone who seemed to know you. Her mind was a blank. She returned to the living room and handed the girl a glass of water.

"So, how are you doing?"

"Good. I hope this water has less chlorine in it than the water at the Community Center pool," the stranger chuckled.

Suddenly the pieces fit together. She remembered the girl clearly.

"You look great, Mandy," Bina smiled. "How did that summer lifeguard job turn out?"

"It was crazy. There I was, fresh out of our lifesaving class, and I was responsible for ten uniquely bratty seven-year-olds."

Bina remembered accidentally pushing Mandy into the pool one day. After that, they had become chummy during the remaining weeks of the training course but had lost touch afterwards.

"Bina, I wish this was just a social call to catch up on old swim class memories, but it's not," Mandy sighed. "I'm here to ask for a favor."

"Sure, what's up?"

"You have to help my mom."

"Your mom?" Bina asked, puzzled.

"Maybe you never made the connection, but I'm Mrs. Palanchio's daughter."

"No way!" Bina sputtered. "I never would have associated you with her. Wait, that came out all wrong," she fumbled, "but you know what I mean."

"Don't worry, I do. My mother remarried so we have different last names. The important thing is that my mom has been hearing things...she says the students think she stole the money. She is so upset and with my sister Theresa's wedding coming up and all, my mom is going nuts." The girl was nearly in tears. "Here, look." She thrust a savings account book into Bina's hand.

"Mandy, you don't have to show me..."

"You see?" Mandy continued as if Bina had not spoken. "My mom saved up over six thousand dollars. It was supposed to be for her retirement so at first, she didn't want to spend it on a big wedding. But Theresa and I kept bugging her. She finally gave in, on the day of the robbery."

Bina nodded sympathetically.

"My mom is falling apart over the implied accusations. She has always loved working at Miami High. Every day she would come home with a different story about how good and caring everyone is. She always says, 'we can learn a lot from religious Jews'. And now that she feels that she is being falsely accused, she is shattered."

Bina would never have guessed that the secretary harbored any good will towards anyone at Miami High. Her outward behavior did not reflect that. If everyone at school would know that their conduct made such an impact on a person, I'd bet they would be more careful, Bina thought.

"I'll talk to the girls, Mandy," Bina said. "And I'm really, really sorry."

"Thanks a ton." Mandy stood up. "I'm sure glad I met you at the Community Center. Who would have known that our chance meeting would be so important to me one day?"

"G-d did."

Mandy looked at her oddly. "Whatever you say, Bina."

When she was gone, Bina grabbed the recipe file and her sweater and dashed out the door.

Mrs. Palanchio was innocent! Now she just had to convince everyone else of that.

As she rounded the corner of the school, Karen Richter was riding up to Chimley's Kosher Chewies on a brand new bicycle.

"Hey, Karen, aren't you coming to school to help us bake?" Bina called. "Why are you going to Chimley's instead?"

"Mind your own business, Bina," Karen snapped. "Keep your nose out of other people's affairs. Got it?"

Chapter Six

Bina flew into Miami High's kitchen and threaded her way through the chaos. Baking pans clattered onto counters and tables. Cartons of eggs and bags of flour were being passed around.

"Sugar. Is there an extra bag of sugar?"

"Where's the measuring cup?"

"Does anyone have a recipe for chocomulas?"

"Go ask Chimley."

A round of laughter rippled through the room.

Heading straight towards Shira, Bina shouted, "You won't believe what just happened. Mrs. Palanchio is innocent!"

All noises stopped. Her classmates froze at the announcement.

"Her daughter, Mandy, just came to my house with proof that it was Mrs. Palanchio's own money and not ours that she is spending on the wedding." After explaining about the bankbook and relating the secretary's feelings about them, Bina glared at everyone. "I'm so glad that none of us even thought of accusing the wrong person!"

"So, Busybody Bina, have you found out who did take our money?" Goldie demanded.

"No."

"Then we had better get back to work, hadn't we?" Goldie smirked. "Or, like, we may never get to shop at Bloomingdale's."

"That's really super news, Bina," Shira said softly, "but Goldie's right. We still have no idea who took the money. And even the cake auction will not raise enough to cover all the missing money."

Bina's euphoria deflated. She was satisfied that the girls seemed to realize that Mrs. Palanchio was not the guilty one, but they were right...they were still no closer to going to New York.

She walked to the kitchen's back window and stared out into the parking area connecting the school and the bakery. Chimley's was buzzing with activity and it was almost an hour past its seven o'clock closing time.

Shira sauntered over to her side.

"Hey, maybe we can ask Chimley for a donation," Bina said, glancing at Shira.

"What on earth are you talking about?"

"Check it out, Shira. Did you ever imagine that Chimley's Chewies had such ritzy customers?" Bina pointed to the three red sports cars parked near Chimley's back entrance. "Two of those cars look like Porsches and the other a Ferrari."

"Amazing," Shira breathed. "What are they doing there?"

"Do you think they're buying pastries?"

"At eight o'clock at night?" Shira asked incredulously. "That's hard to believe but then again, you and I can testify to how delicious Chimley's cakes are. Maybe those rich guys get cravings for sweets late at night."

Bina tugged Shira down below window

level.

"They're coming out," Bina whispered.

"They can't hear us," Shira whispered back.

"Somehow I don't think they would like it if they saw us watching them."

"How do you know that?"

"I don't know, but why are they wearing sunglasses at night? Maybe they don't want to be recognized."

"Why are you crouching down on the floor?" Ariella tapped Bina on the shoulder and without waiting for an answer, continued, "We need your help with the chocomulas. They're slipping and sliding all over the place."

"Duty calls," Bina sighed and went to rescue the pastries.

Two Nursery girls, Aviva and Estee, were attempting to lift a thin sheet of rolled chocolate dough when Bina and Ariella approached.

"What's up, Rosenthal?" Bina said jokingly to Estee. "You too worried about keeping your nails pretty to touch the dough?"

"I think there's too much shortening in here," Estee wailed. "It keeps slipping away."

Known to all as a master baker, Bina looked at the dough with a baker's seasoned eye and made her prognosis.

"Maybe we can dry it up with a little more flour and confectionery sugar."

When the problem was finally solved, the friends cut and layered the white and dark chocolate alternately while Bina worked on her own unique creation.

"I'm glad Mrs. Palanchio is no longer a suspect," Estee said. "I was talking to my sister last night and she didn't think it was her either."

"Yeah, I felt such pity for the woman," Aviva added. "She's no friend of mine but I didn't think she would do it either. I'm beginning to think that maybe it was someone in our class."

"You're not the only one," Estee interjected.

"You think I did it?" Bina asked, unbelievingly.

"Oh, come on Bina, of course not."

Estee waved her hand dismissively. "What I mean to say is you have to be deaf not to hear who others are talking about."

"Now wait a minute! We just got through falsely accusing Mrs. Palanchio," Bina pleaded. "Don't start this again."

"The difference between falsely accusing Mrs. Palanchio and the person we're talking about is that Mrs. Palanchio was obviously innocent," Ariella explained patiently, "whereas Karen Richter appears to be guilty."

"Proof one," Estee said quickly. "Look who is the only one not here baking with us tonight."

"Proof two, look who wasn't the least bit excited about the trip from the beginning," Ariella added.

"And proof three," Aviva concluded, "look who has a spanking-new, super-elite bicycle just a few days after the robbery."

Goldie, passing the Nursery girls' table on her way to the sink, overheard part of their conversation and gladly put in her two-cents-worth. "I agree. I think Karen Richter did it and it's probably just a matter of time before she'll do something like it again. I really don't feel safe around her. It's like being in class with a criminal." She shuddered and walked away in a huff.

Bina was fuming. How unfair to accuse a classmate.

"Just because we're not friends with Karen, doesn't mean we can say bad things about her," Bina scolded. "You know, and I know, that when the trip was announced not everyone was enthusiastic. As far as not being here now, I just saw Karen going into Chimley's. Evidently she had to work tonight. And, I hate to break it to you, but I've sometimes gotten a new bike without stealing money."

"Bina, calm down," Estee soothed. "I thought some of our observations might be helpful. Since you uncovered the true story about Mrs. Palanchio, I thought maybe you could discover the real culprit if you knew all the nitty-gritty particulars. Don't be angry, okay?"

"Okay, but don't go around accusing Karen. It's just not right."

Bina decided it was time to change the

subject. "Let's see if the chocomulas are finished." Donning oven mitts, she opened the oven door and slid the tray out.

"They look and smell scrumptious," Estee gushed.

After everyone's baked goods were cooling, Bina and Shira initiated a massive clean up. There were flour drifts, egg shells and empty containers everywhere. It took five garbage bags to hold the baking night's refuse.

"Everyone, thanks for your help," said Shira, loading her garbage bag into a trash can. "See you tomorrow. Tell all your friends and relatives and remind them to bid, bid, bid and buy, buy, buy!"

When everyone left, Shira and Bina stood by the window.

"Bina, how much money do you think we'll make tomorrow?"

"I doubt if we'll pass the thousand dollar mark."

"You sound upset."

"I am. It's so disappointing to hear that some girls put finding the money before decency to other people."

"You're talking about Mrs. Palanchio and now Karen?"

"Yes."

"Some girls do seem to think it's Karen," Shira agreed.

Bina sat down on a stool amid a cornucopia of desserts. On the left were a towering pile of chocomulas. A batch of blueberry muffins ran over the top of a wicker basket on the right, prevented from toppling by extra layers of Saran Wrap. The wealth of goodies was dizzying to behold, but they could not distract Bina from her preoccupation with Karen Richter.

"But their so-called proofs aren't very impressive."

"There is something a little odd about Karen's behavior," Shira said, glancing out of the window. "Hey, look," she pointed outside. Bina jumped up.

Three luxury cars screeched to a stop. Two men jumped out of each car and slithered into Chimley's back entrance.

"I don't understand it," Bina shook her head. "What could be at Chimley's to make the owners of such expensive cars want to go there after hours?"

"Do you think it's the caramel-pecan rolls?" Shira giggled.

"Somehow, I don't believe that the rolls are the motivating factor," Bina chuckled. "It doesn't seem logical that these guys, sitting in their mansions, crave Chimley's food enough to come out at night...wearing their sunglasses, no less."

One by one each car sped off into the darkness.

"Shira, they are definitely not going to Chimley's for the food."

"How can you tell?"

"The flat boxes they each carried out were not high enough to hold Chimley's baked goods." Bina turned away from the window. "Let's call it a night. I'm exhausted."

"Me too," Shira yawned and reached for her sweater.

Bina walked to the table and gathered her recipes. "I'll ask Karen tomorrow. Maybe she'll know why these guys come to Chimley's after hours."

They closed the lights, set the alarm and

locked the school doors.

"Speaking of the devil, look, there's Karen," Bina whispered.

"I can't believe she works so late."

"Karen!" Bina called.

Karen jumped when she heard her name.

"It's me, Bina, with Shira." They walked up to her.

"Oh, hi," Karen mumbled.

"Chimley must be some sort of slave boss, making you work so late," Bina began. "I never knew his store was such a happening place so late at night."

"Well, now you know," Karen sneered. "Excuse me, I'm going home."

"Why is Chimley here at this hour?"

"Not that it's any of your business, Bina, but Chimley has poker games at night. I came in to catch up on the bookkeeping."

"Chimley must bet big money to gather such a wealthy group—and on a weeknight, too," Bina said, trying to squeeze more information out of her.

"Listen, I stay in the front of the store, they stay in the back. I don't ask questions," Karen mounted her bike, "and if you were smart, you'd do the same." She rode off before Bina could say another word.

"That went well," Shira said dryly. "I don't think she enjoyed her interview."

"I won't win any popularity contests with her, that's for sure," Bina shrugged. "Chimley's light is still on. The poker game must still be going on."

They made their way to the Gold residence. In their tired state, they appreciated that it was only two short blocks away.

Shira fell asleep immediately but Bina tossed and turned. After hearing the grandfather clock in the living room strike two, Bina climbed out of bed. She rubbed her eyes, put on her robe and tiptoed out of the room.

In her father's study, she looked around the comfortable, cream-colored room. Piles of books and papers were everywhere...on the desk, the window sills, the floor.

Bina settled back into her father's chair behind the desk, her mind trying to make sense of everything. As much as she tried to reject the thought, a nagging doubt lingered: someone from her class could have taken the money. If ruining the trip for the rest of the class was not the thief's intention, maybe it was the need for cash.

On a table against the wall was the gleaming new computer that Bina had begged her father to purchase. She not only knew how to use it, but was also adept at writing programs. She was elected president of the local computer club because of her expertise in the subject.

She went to the computer and downloaded her class list onto the screen. Scanning the names, she reviewed the Goods first. Without too much deliberation, she deleted them one by one. Their standards of goodness and self-sacrifice were too high to even imagine that one of them could do such a thing. More than that, however, was their dedication to Jewish values. The prohibitions against stealing would keep them from dipping into class funds.

Then she began scanning the others. She erased each girl for one plausible reason or another. There were only a few names left. The Nursery girls. She knew them so well. Bina had been with them through some rough times, like when one had been caught cheating on a test or, another, for cutting class. Bina could recognize their guilty expressions in an instant. None had been wearing the face of wrongdoing lately. She deleted their names.

One name remained. Karen Richter.

She stared at the screen. Karen Richter, the loner. Karen Richter, the angry one. Karen Richter, working late at Chimley's. Karen had no friends. The thought of ruining the convention for everyone would not have bothered her. Maybe Karen's family desperately needed the money.

"I have no proof," Bina said sadly to the computer screen. "A list is nothing."

The computer screen became fuzzy and the letters seemed to droop like melted wax. She sat back and closed her eyes. The room ceased its swirling as Bina began to decide what to do next.

Tomorrow, she decided. Tomorrow she would confront Karen. Bina's stomach churned anxiously, with the possibility of, what if...?

Chapter Seven

"Shira, I have to go to the school library," Bina said, the next day after the noon bell rang. Crowds of people were making their way to the lunchroom for the start of the bake sale. "If the pecan rolls come up for auction before I get back, please buy one for me, okay?"

"What about that diet you said you were starting?" Shira teased.

"You're right. Buy two for me. I don't want to get too thin."

"Atta girl." Shira took Bina's money, grabbed her lunch and headed for the door. "Hurry back."

The library was dark, thick curtains covering the windows. On the desk, a lone lamp was lit, casting eerie shadows over the stacks of books. Bina went to the desk where her history teacher had left a book she needed for a report. While flipping through the pages, Bina heard a sound. She froze.

"Is someone here?"

A sniffle, followed by a hiccup, answered her.

She attempted to peer into the library's darkness. No one seemed to be there. The tables were clean; the chairs were empty.

Another sniffle. It seemed to be coming from the far corner of the room. Bina tiptoed towards the sound. She saw someone crouched between the books on food and fossils.

"Karen!" Bina gulped. "Are you okay?"

"Yes," came the shaky response from the crumpled girl.

"Are you sure?" Bina hesitated. Her overtures towards Karen had not gone well before, to put it mildly.

"Yes." There was a pause, and then a barely audible, "No."

"Here, have some of my muffin."

Karen looked at Bina, her eyes welling up with tears, threatening to spill over onto her cheeks.

"Why are you offering me food?"

"I don't know," Bina laughed uncertainly. "I guess whenever I'm upset, I feel better after I eat something."

"That's not a very healthy reaction. You will turn into a blimp if you eat every time you're upset."

"You're right, but I drink diet soda to balance the calories. I figure if I'm inflated by food, I'll be deflated by asparetame."

Karen sighed, "I don't think it will work."

"Neither do I." Bina was surprised at Karen's civility. She was almost being friendly. "Karen, I don't think you should be sitting on the floor. It's awfully dirty."

"I guess you're right." But she made no attempt to move. "I thought this was a good place to...to..." Karen's voice trailed off as she dissolved into tears.

"A good place to be miserable alone?" Bina waited but Karen didn't answer. "Do you want to talk about it?"

"You wouldn't understand and why would you care?"

"Does there have to be a reason?" Bina slid down onto the dusty floor. "You are a human being, not to mention my classmate, and you are upset. Why shouldn't I care?"

"No one has since I came to this school, so why start now?"

Now that sounded like the bitter and whiny Karen that Bina was used to.

"Well, I hate to say this," Bina began, "and I don't want to be mean, but whenever someone tries to talk to you, you totally brush them off. You push people away."

"Maybe that's because there are many things bothering me. I am not always up to being nice."

"I feel that way too sometimes," Bina sympathized.

"I don't think you can even begin to imagine how I feel," Karen shot back.

"Maybe I can't but this is exactly why people don't bother talking to you. Your abrupt manner is hurtful."

"Listen Bina, I'd say I was sorry if I would mean it, but I don't." Karen's voice rose with fierceness, "Why should I apologize to you, one of the people who have been making my life miserable?"

"Before you continue, Karen, think, for a second, if you really want to talk to me like this," Bina said coldly. "I have been going out of my way trying to make amends. I have to tell you, it hasn't been easy."

"What do you want, a medal?"

"No. I don't think you understand my point at all." Bina tried to remain calm. "I am trying to be friendly. I am willing to listen to you and if I can help in any way, I will."

There was a long pause.

"It's so hard," Karen's tone softened. "It's so depressing not to have anyone to talk to."

Bina said nothing.

"It's hard to see everyone except me with a group of friends, you know?"

"Yeah," Bina answered softly.

"You can't know what it's like to feel you have no one. You are a Nursery girl, so you have a close circle of friends." Karen wiped her eyes with a crumpled tissue. "When I first came to this school, I was so upset about moving here and leaving the old neighborhood, my school and all my friends.

"My father's firm had transferred him from Orlando to Miami and we had to move, but I refused to accept it." Karen blew her nose. "I realize now that I acted like a big baby, but at the time, I was determined not to like it here. I kept to myself, sulking, ignoring any overtures of friendship. And after a while, everyone left me alone." She looked down at her hands.

"By the time I was ready to make friends, a pattern had been established and everyone just ignored me. And I became bitter all over again. But at least I had a warm, happy family to go home to every day. At least until lately."

"What happened to change that?" Bina asked.

Karen leaned her head back against the wall. Her eyes had a faraway look.

"First my father and then my mother got laid off from work. Everybody's company is downsizing, trimming costs. Now, my parents are on edge all the time. Every little thing bothers them. They storm around the house yelling and screaming. My older sister and I end up doing practically everything in the house because they are either going to endless job interviews or are too stressed out to care about anything." She seemed to forget that Bina was there. "It's hard when things are going badly but it seems to me that they should have more *bitachon*, faith in *Hashem's* master plan. Things are bound to get better soon."

"Why do you think they are acting this way?" Bina changed her position. It was uncomfortable sitting on the hard floor.

"I think that they have given up hope. The pressure is just building and building and they're reacting badly to it. They refuse to ask anyone for monetary help or to even let anyone know what bad shape we are in. They are afraid that people will think less of them or something."

"Isn't there anyone you can turn to for help?"

"No. No one would care. They might

understand why I'm so grumpy lately, but they wouldn't help."

"Maybe that's how your parents feel. Maybe they also feel no one can help them."

"Maybe, but in their case, they are wrong. If they told someone, like, I don't know, like the welfare department, then maybe..." Karen's head snapped forward, her eyes coming back into focus. "Oh my G-d," she gasped, horrified. "I can't believe I told you all this. My parents will kill me. What a big mouth I have!"

"No you don't."

"Oh, why did I shoot my stupid mouth off?"

"Maybe because you finally realized that I could be your friend," Bina said softly. "And friends tell each other things."

"You are a real cornball," Karen said uncomfortably, trying to diffuse the intensity of the moment with humor.

"Yep, that's me." Bina stood up and dusted off her skirt. "But I mean it, Karen, you can talk to me anytime. However, right now, it's lunch and bake sale time, so let's get out of here. I'm starving and Shira promised to buy two pecan rolls for me."

"Can I exchange the muffin offer for one of those pecan rolls?" Karen asked hopefully.

Bina laughed. "Sure thing, pal."

Bina and Karen turned more than a few heads when they entered the auditorium together, where the bake auction was in full swing.

"Okay, everybody," Shira, as auctioneer, was saying. "Open your hearts and your wallets for this batch of delicious blueberry muffins. Believe me, your stomachs will thank you. The bidding will start at four dollars."

As the bids rang out from the audience, Bina observed her classmates' expressions...a mixture of hope and doubt.

After dinner that evening, Bina sat on her bed, looking through the history book that she had taken from the school library. She flipped to the index at the back searching for a reference to her topic.

"Bina, Estee's on the phone," her mother called from the kitchen.

"Okay, thanks Mom." Bina reached over to her night table and picked up the receiver.

"Hi, Estee, what's up?"

"Do I have news for you!" Estee sang out. "You won't believe what Aviva and I saw on the way home from school today."

"What?"

"Well, Aviva and I were walking home and we passed Collins Avenue, like we always do."

"Yes?"

"You know Karen lives on Collins."

"Really?" Bina sighed.

"Yeah, so we were walking by Karen's house when we saw the strangest thing. Did you know that her kitchen faces the street?"

"No." Bina wished Estee would get to the point. She had lots of work to do.

"Well, it does. Anyway, through the window we saw Karen trying to pry open a box. She was banging it against the counter. When that didn't work, she took what looked like a screwdriver and opened it."

"Why are you telling me this?"

"Have patience, my friend!" Estee chided. "Aviva and I really got interested when Karen emptied the box. It was filled with money."

"It was probably a *tzedakah* box so of course it would be filled with money," Bina replied testily. "Maybe Karen was totaling the amount to send to charity."

"That's what we thought too, until we saw Karen pocketing the money. Then she came outside. Aviva asked her where she was going and Karen said she was going to the store to buy some things."

"So?" Bina said irritably.

"So maybe if Karen would stoop so low as to steal money from charity, then maybe she would have no qualms about taking our convention money."

"Estee! I thought we agreed not to..."

"Listen Bina," Estee interrupted. "I have to go do my homework. I just thought you should know every little thing so you can decide if things are adding up. You know, if Karen's guilty or not. You're so good at figuring things out. Bye."

The connection was broken before Bina

could utter a sound.

Bina agonized over Estee's intimations. Everyone seems so sure that Karen is the thief. Is it just *loshon hora* or justified doubts? Bina didn't know what to do. She needed some unbiased, intelligent advice.

So she called a family council meeting.

Chapter Eight

"Family council meeting in the dining room, please," Bina called. She waited. No one came. "Family council meeting is starting now," she repeated loudly. Nothing.

She dashed into the kitchen.

"Dad, I called a family council meeting."

Her father shut the faucet.

"Sorry Bina, I didn't hear you with the water running. Washing greasy dishes is a noisy process."

Bina nodded and pointed in the direction of the dining room.

"I need you now," she pleaded.

"Yes, ma'am. This sounds serious. I'll just set this pot to soak and I'll be right there."

Bina spun on her heels and headed toward the study where her mother was doing homework. She knocked on the door. Since she felt this was an emergency, Bina didn't feel so guilty about disturbing her mother's study hour.

Family council meetings were a relatively new innovation in the Gold household, something her mother's professor had said was a surefire way to improve family communication. The meetings were always requested by her parents in order to make an announcement or discuss a family problem. They were always held in the dining room. Bina was not usually enthusiastic about them, but this time was different.

As her parents sat down at the table, Mrs. Gold said, "Yossi is at a friend's house."

"That's okay. I really just need both of you anyway." Bina ran a hand through her hair. "I'm sorry I barged in on you like this, but this is kind of urgent. Can we skip the old business and go directly to the new?"

Bina's parents exchanged a surprised look.

"Sure," her mother said.

Bina began by bringing them up-to-date about the missing money saga.

"Are there any suspects?" Rabbi Gold asked.

"Yes...maybe...I dunno..." Bina swallowed hard. "Some of the girls think it is one of our classmates," Bina said miserably. "We don't really have proof, but there are some things that seem to point to her."

"Perhaps you should discuss this with your principal," her father suggested.

"That's a good idea," Bina's mother agreed. "Mrs. Schaeffer is very good at resolving school problems."

"But what if I'm wrong?" Bina cried. "What if she's innocent?"

"Well, maybe you should tell Mrs. Schaeffer what you think," her mother encouraged. "Then she could do her own investigation."

"I dunno..." Bina mumbled.

Everyone sat quietly, thinking.

"How about confronting the girl

directly," her father said, finally. "Not with accusations, but as a friend."

Bina mulled over this suggestion.

Rabbi Gold added, "I'd be happy to drive you there anytime, if you should decide..."

"Dad," Bina jumped up, "I'll take you up on your offer. Can we go now?"

"Right now?" Her father was taken aback. "Well, sure, if you'd like..."

"I'll just look up her address. Be back in a sec."

Bina returned with a handful of cookies. "Just thought I might need some food for courage," she grinned.

The cranky old station wagon took three tries before its engine roared to life. Bina's anxiety mounted as they backed out of the driveway. She told her father about the problems in Karen's home.

"Dad, do you know anybody who could give Karen's father a job?"

"Do you know what his skills are?"

"I don't know, but maybe, while I talk with Karen, you could casually discuss it with him."

"I don't see why not. Maybe he could

help out in the yeshiva," he suggested.

"It's real important that he shouldn't know that Karen told me anything."

Her father nodded.

All too soon, the Gold mobile chugged onto Karen Richter's street. As she looked at the houses for the address, Bina felt the hairs on the back of her neck prickle. She had no script, no preparation for what she should say. She mouthed a prayer for success and guidance.

Bina took a deep breath as she stood by the front door. She knocked softly. When no one answered, she was relieved. Maybe they weren't home. Maybe this wasn't such a good idea, after all.

The door swung open and there stood Karen.

"Bina! What are you doing here?" a surprised Karen asked, her eyes sliding from Bina to Rabbi Gold and back to Bina again.

"I...I have to talk to you. Can we come in?"

"Sure." She stepped aside to let them enter.

"Can we talk privately in your room?"

Bina asked. When Karen nodded, Bina added, "Is your father home? Maybe he can keep my dad company while he's waiting for me."

"Sure," Karen said again but didn't sound sure at all. "He's in the kitchen giving my little sister a bedtime snack. Come, I'll introduce you."

In the bedroom, Karen's older sister Sara was dramatically reciting a Shakespeare soliloquy. She was a freshman at the local community college. After introductions were made, Bina glanced around the unkempt room. The beds were unmade and there was a pile of dirty laundry on the floor.

"Could you please practice in another room?" Karen asked.

"But, Karen, I just got here," Sara moaned melodramatically.

"C'mon Sara. Please. I'll make it up to you."

With a deep sigh, Sara sashayed out the door, saying, "Remember now, you owe me one."

"I'm sure you're wondering why I'm here," Bina began with a quaking voice as soon as the door closed.

"You could say that."

"Let's sit down, okay?" It was hard to remain standing because her knees were shaking. She sank onto the edge of the bed.

"You know, I was so excited when they announced that we could go to the Bais Yaakov Convention in New York. Then they told us that it was going to cost three hundred and fifty dollars and I wasn't sure if everyone could come up with so much money." Bina paused, her hand idly straightening the wrinkles in the bedsheet. "But somehow, everyone did. Except you. I didn't mention that I knew you didn't pay because I didn't want to embarrass you, in case you didn't have the money. I thought funds in the student council's account could cover your cost if it was a problem for you. But then, all the money was gone."

Bina looked out the window and said softly, "Karen, I have to ask this. Did you take it?"

Karen jumped up as if she had sat on a thumbtack. "Get out!" she shouted. "Now! Before I physically throw you out." Her hands flailed angrily in the air. "I can't believe you! Some friend you are. I don't ever want to see your face again!"

"Karen, listen, we all make mistakes. It's okay, I won't tell anyone."

"Didn't you hear me?" Karen screamed. "Out! Or are you deaf? I didn't take the money. Boy, was I a fool to trust you with my problems, you backstabbing, lying, story-telling hypocrite!"

"Now you just hold on there a minute." Bina leaped to her feet indignantly. "I didn't decide to ask you because of what you told me. That has nothing whatever to do with this conversation." Then, without thinking, she blurted out, "And what about the money you took from the *tzedakah* box this afternoon?"

Karen gasped, her eyes narrowing into a piercing glare.

"How did you know about that?"

"Some of the girls, passing by your house, saw you and told me," Bina admitted sheepishly.

"You have really sunk to a new low, Bina Gold," Karen hissed through gritted teeth. "Having people spy on me?"

"I didn't ask anyone to spy on..."

But Karen didn't hear her; she was so wrapped up in her own fury. "Before starting to play detective, why didn't you just come to me and ask?" Karen snarled. "Yes I took money from the *tzedakah* box. I figured my family was just as needy as those we've been collecting for. Maybe it wasn't the best thing to do, but I had no choice. We had no money for food." Tears were streaming down her face. "I didn't touch the convention money. I give you my word on that."

Bina was moved by the vehement denial, but still..."How could you afford to buy a new bike?"

"What? That ugly bike?" Karen laughed painfully. "My sister Sara won it in a raffle that she entered in a drugstore. She gave it to me because she just got her driver's license."

Ashen-faced, Bina collapsed on the bed and buried her head in her hands.

"I am so sorry," she murmured hoarsely. "How could I have been so stupid? Here I have been preaching to everyone not to make false accusations, and I go ahead and do just that." Tears filled Bina's eyes. "What can I do to make it up to you?"

"Bina, stop crying." Karen fidgeted awkwardly. "You're getting my sheets all wet."

"What a fool I am," Bina mumbled. "I thought I was Sherlock Holmes. I feel awful. Please say that you forgive me. I'll leave immediately."

"Bina, quit it, will you? I can't handle this apology scene," Karen sighed and pulled Bina to her feet. "If you want to find the missing money, you're wasting your time here."

"Do you forgive me?" Bina pleaded.

"No. Not yet. That was a pretty terrible thing you did," Karen said reproachfully. "But I've done some pretty terrible things myself and I wouldn't like it if they were held against me forever." Karen handed Bina a tissue. "If you wanted help finding the money, why didn't you just ask?"

"Can you help?"

"I don't know," she shrugged, "but it

seems to me that one thing you should do is examine the crime scene."

"How would that help? Knowing Mrs. Palanchio, I'm sure that everything is back in place."

"Yes, but maybe, by retracing your steps, you might remember something important that had slipped your mind."

Bina followed Karen out of the bedroom, still feeling uneasy about her earlier behavior.

"By the way, why is your dad here?"

"He drove me here and is waiting to take me home. But in the meantime, he's talking to your father about a job."

"What?!" Karen staggered backwards. "Oh, no! How could you do that, Bina? That was a private conversation. My father is going to kill me for talking about our problems. This is terrible."

"Karen, as a principal, my father deals with parents everyday and it's not uncommon for people to ask him about jobs."

"But my father didn't ask him about a job," Karen spat out. "He will be so furious and when he gets mad, boy, just stay clear of him."

Bina and Karen went to the kitchen where their fathers were sitting at the table, talking.

"Bina," Rabbi Gold smiled, "Mr. Richter's cousin and I went to yeshiva together. Small world, huh?" Looking at Karen, he continued smoothly, "Your father was telling me that he used to work for the telephone company. We were discussing the latest boom in the cellular phone industry." Rabbi Gold smiled at Mr. Richter. "I know a few people in the business and I recall them kvetching about how hard it is to find good repairmen. I'll speak to them about you."

"It would be great to work in the telephone field again," Mr. Richter said. "I am dreading a job in a factory."

"Dad, I'll be ready to leave in a few minutes," Bina said as the girls went into the foyer.

"Boy, your father is a miracle-worker," Karen breathed. "I can't believe that my father isn't angry."

"Not a miracle-worker, but he is a very special person," Bina said proudly. "Now let's figure out how we can get into the school tonight."

"Tonight?" Karen's eyes opened wide. "Haven't you had enough excitement for one night?"

"No way," Bina declared. "I happen to think that your idea about checking out the crime scene is an excellent one. And we can't do it during the day with the all-seeing, all-knowing Mrs. Palanchio around."

"Well, good luck and good-bye."

"Karen, you have to come with me."

"Why?"

"Because I get the feeling that if I had consulted with you in the first place, I would have avoided this whole mess," Bina explained. "I don't want to make the same mistake twice. Besides, you can't tell me that you aren't hooked on finding out who did it."

Karen thought a moment.

"Fine, but how are we going to get inside the school at this hour? Or do your talents also include the ability to open the school's locks and crack the burglar alarm?"

"No, but I know who can. Shira." Bina grinned triumphantly. "She has been working late on a student council project and Mrs. Schaeffer gave her a set of keys and showed her how to override the alarm."

Karen looked at Bina with admiration and handed her the telephone receiver.

"What's this for?" Bina asked.

"I don't suppose you communicate with Shira telepathically, do you? I'll dial. You talk."

Chapter Nine

"Are you sure you will be safe here?"
Bina's father said, as the girls got out of the
station wagon.

"Yes, Dad. Don't worry, it's not late.
Please tell mom that I'll be sleeping at
Shira's tonight. Okay?"

He drove away just as Shira arrived.

"Hi, Karen." Karen acknowledged her
with a grunt.

Shira looked at Bina. "What's this all
about?"

"As I told you on the phone, Karen had
a great idea."

"So you said. What's the great idea and
why are we here at school?"

"She thought we should check out the
crime scene."

Shira winked at Karen. "Now there's a girl with a head on her shoulders. Let's go."

Her fingers nimbly pecked out the alarm code and with a turn of the key, Miami High's door was open.

"This place is spooky at night." Bina shivered as they entered the school.

"Not to mention smelly," Karen added.

"Maybe the janitor didn't come in today. Hey, have you considered him as a suspect?" Shira joked. "He always looked a little shifty to me."

"The janitor only comes in after school hours and the money was stolen during the day," Bina noted dryly.

"You really are serious about this, aren't you. Well, don't let little ole me get in the way of a great mastermind."

"Don't be offended. It's just that I don't want to get sidetracked with off-the-wall ideas."

The fluorescent lights flickered as Karen turned them on. They squinted as their eyes adjusted to the light.

"Okay now, if I remember correctly, I had come down the hall right after the lunch bell sounded. I was so excited. The idea of going to New York had made my head spin. By the time I reached the office, I was way off in daydream land. I opened the desk drawer and the money was not there. My heart and stomach did a flip flop. I remember that clearly. Then I searched on top and under the desk too."

"Do you remember anything out of the ordinary?" Shira asked.

"I don't think so. Although I admit that my memory, especially when I am fantasizing, has never been one of my strong points."

"That's just great," Karen snapped. "So why are we bothering to do this at all? If you can't remember anything, then this is useless. It's just about as useful as you having people spying on me."

Shira's head spun around. "What do you mean? Bina didn't have people spying on you."

Bina looked embarrassed. "I didn't but somebody did."

Bina told Shira about Estee's phone call earlier, without mentioning names, and then what had happened at Karen's house.

Uncomfortable with these disclosures, Shira changed the subject. "Let's go into the office." She unlocked the door and switched on the lights.

"Karen, let's try to help Bina remember." Shira closed her eyes. "Let's see. I remember that on the day the money was stolen, I had cut my finger in class and Mrs. Schaeffer bandaged it for me."

"Right, maybe there is hope because I remember that too," Bina laughed. "I also recall that Mrs. Schaeffer couldn't find Mrs. Palanchio and she took the first-aid kit back to the office herself."

"How could you not find Mrs. Palanchio?" Karen snickered. "What was she doing, hiding in the supply closet?"

"She was probably measuring the chalk pieces so she could figure out if a teacher was using too much."

Shira joined in, mimicking the secretary's New York accent, "'You teachers, I know what you are doing...trying to trick me...what kind of teacher would actually use chalk in a classroom?'"

They giggled helplessly.

"One thing you have to say for Mrs. Palanchio, though, she is very neat..." Bina stopped suddenly. "Hey...wait, I remember something now."

"This is a moment to remember," Karen drawled.

"No, really. I had completely forgotten. Mrs. Palanchio's desk was a big mess the day of the robbery. It looked a lot like my desk at home. All of her papers were scattered about, her desk calendar and phone number file were out of place."

"Mrs. Palanchio must have been having a rebellious day," Shira teased. "All that neatness must have gone to her head and she freaked out on the day of the robbery. Or maybe she was trying out a new image, 'the messy-desk look'."

Karen and Shira laughed until they noticed that Bina was silently pacing, looking very serious.

"Now that I think about it, this could be our first true-to-life clue," Bina said thoughtfully. "Mrs. Palanchio would never leave her desk like that. Her desk is like her castle."

"Yeah. I remember that. Mrs. Palanchio had been furious about that," Shira said. "Remember that sign she posted on the door warning that anyone going even close to her desk would be severely punished?"

"Someone had searched through her desk looking for something that day," Bina said slowly. "Probably the person who took the money."

"But who?" Shira asked impatiently.

"How should I know?" Bina snapped and resumed pacing. Karen followed her. Within moments all three were pacing one behind the other. Shira was the first to giggle.

"I've got it!" Bina shouted. "It must be that whoever took the money was a stranger. Everyone who knew about the money also knew where I had put it. They wouldn't have had to rummage through the desk to find it."

Shira cheered.

"We still don't know who the thief is," Karen said soberly, "so save your applause for later."

"You're right," Shira frowned.

"Bina, do you remember who had been in the office when you left the money there?" Karen asked.

"Yes. Chimley, Mrs. Solomon, Mrs. Palanchio and the photocopier repair guy."

"I can't believe you didn't have to spy on them to figure out that they were innocent," Karen complained. "Why was I the only lucky one?"

Bina grimaced. "Let's try to see the robbery from the thief's point of view," she suggested, ignoring Karen's comment. "Maybe that will help." She walked to the desk. "Shira, do you have the key to Mrs. Palanchio's desk drawers?"

"I might." Shira rapidly fished through Mrs. Schaeffer's key ring until she found the familiar purple-headed key that Mrs. Palanchio always used. "This looks like it."

"Bina, how will it help if you open the drawer?" Karen was skeptical. "I hate to break the news to you, but the money is long gone. So if you're hoping to miraculously find it, you would have better luck searching my house again."

Bina took a deep breath. Karen will never let me live this down. She had hoped that including Karen in the search for the money would ease tensions between them.

"I want the re-enactment to be as realistic as possible," Bina mumbled. "Okay, I'll play the thief."

She moved to the door and, facing the room, started to narrate her actions.

"I am going into the office. Well how about that, Mrs. Palanchio isn't here...so this is a good time to steal some cash." She walked past the copy machine into the center of the office. "But since I don't know where the money is, I am going to look under some of Mrs. Palanchio's papers, move her calendar and records around."

Nothing was coming to her. It was frustrating but she kept trying.

"So, here I am at the desk. I will look in the drawers, starting with the bottom one. I stick in my hand and pull out...oh, gross!"

Shira squinted. "What's wrong?"

"I just found a chewed-up toothpick in the drawer. How disgusting. What's a toothpick doing here?"

"Maybe Mrs. Palanchio picks her teeth when no one's looking," Shira grinned.

Karen was staring at the bent toothpick, splintered from excessive chewing.

"You know," she said thoughtfully. "I've seen those toothpicks before."

"Who hasn't seen a toothpick before?" Shira retorted.

Karen ignored her. "I find them all over the bakery floor. Chimley is always chewing on them."

"That's right." Bina snapped her fingers. "I never see Chimley without a toothpick in his mouth. Maybe he did it," she said excitedly. "Maybe Jacko Chimley took the money."

Karen glared at her. "When are you going to stop accusing innocent people?" Karen said angrily. "Just because Chimley is a little odd, doesn't mean you can just blame him at will."

"Karen's right," Shira said. "I don't think finding one of his toothpicks here is enough to say he's guilty of stealing the money. Karen said Chimley leaves his toothpicks everywhere. And he comes to the office all the time."

"And besides, you have no idea how nice Chimley is." Karen's voice was filled with indignation. "He's a lot more fair and square than you are. His weights in the bakery are always calibrated with perfect accuracy to give people the exact amount that they are paying for. Chimley didn't have to make the bakery kosher, you know. He told me that he did it because Miami High girls were so refined that he wanted them to be able to eat in his bakery too."

Karen's hands were flying around, emphasizing her fury.

"Do you know that whenever the *mashgiach* comes by unannounced to check on the *kashrus*, Chimley always gives him free pastries to take home? Chimley may be a little strange, but he has a good heart. How dare you accuse him!"

For a long time, everyone stared at the floor without speaking.

"Karen," Bina said finally. "I don't want to accuse Chimley falsely, and maybe I was too hasty in assuming he had taken the money, but I want to point out something."

Bina placed her palms on the desk. "Mrs. Palanchio always keeps her drawers locked, so how would one of Chimley's toothpicks end up in there?"

"If Mrs. Palanchio is so careful about keeping her drawers locked," Karen said sarcastically, "under such tight security, then tell me how Chimley could have possibly gotten to the money in the first place?"

Bina thought about that. "Okay. How about this. When Shira got hurt, Mrs. Palanchio ran with the first-aid kit. What if, in her haste, she forgot to lock the drawer after I put in the money and later just assumed she had done so." Bina pushed her hair off her face. "Chimley is always in here making phone calls and 'borrowing' supplies. Maybe he was scrounging around for something to take."

"That could explain the messy desk," Shira put in.

"Right, and then maybe he hit upon the manila envelope with the money. His mouth must have dropped open at the sight of so much cash."

"So how come Mrs. Palanchio didn't notice the messy desk immediately?" Karen challenged. "She would have had to be dead not to react to that!"

"Well it could have happened after she left the school," Bina theorized. "Or, since she was late for her dressmaker appointment, and Shira's accident made her even later, it's possible that she headed straight to her locker in the staff lounge and never returned to the office at all."

They mulled over those possibilities.

"Fine, a clue is a clue," Karen conceded. "You're forgetting one thing, though. In every crime, there has to be a motive. Why would Chimley take our measly money?"

"First of all, it wasn't measly," Bina shot back. "It was thousands of dollars."

"For Chimley, that amount is measly," Karen countered. "I work at the cash register and you should see the money that pours in. On Thursdays and Fridays alone, people spend tons of money on desserts and things for *Shabbos*. And during the week, the store is always crowded. He makes out very well."

"Not to mention, Bina, that your purchases alone would make him a very rich man," Shira said, in an attempt to lighten the charged atmosphere. "Your pecan roll addiction is funding his American dream."

Bina cracked a weak smile.

"I might also add," Karen said, "that Chimley would not host so many poker games unless he was doing very well in them. You've seen the guys who come there. I suspect that they aren't playing poker for nickels and dimes. In light of all this, I have one recommendation."

"Which is?" Bina sighed.

"Keep your wild accusations to yourself until you know what you're talking about. Or do you want to continue humiliating other people and yourself with your 'so-called' proofs."

The accumulation of Karen's barbs all evening finally got to Bina. She sat down, her temper rising.

"Karen, let's get something clear between us," Bina said, trying to control her emotions. "I am terribly sorry about what I did to you. I feel awful. But if you don't believe that I'm really sorry and won't do it again, then I don't know what else to do." Bina slammed shut the desk drawer. "Please stop constantly throwing my mistake back in my face. It won't help us get past this if you keep rubbing it in."

Bina clenched her fists, simmering with exasperation. "If it's impossible for you to do that, then go home now. I'll pay for the taxi. It's probably my own shortcoming, a lack of patience or whatever, but I can't take any more of your nasty comments." She slid back the chair and stood up. "I really want to try to find the money and go to New York. You have been helpful so far. I want you to stay, but it's your choice."

Karen's shoulders sagged and she lowered her eyes. "Okay. I can't promise that something won't slip out, but I think trying to figure this all out will be exciting. Thanks for including me."

Shira drew an imaginary bow over an imaginary violin and whistled melodramatically. "That was very touching, you guys. I was so moved. Now that we're all friends again, can we return to the problem at hand?"

"Yes. Let's get back to what Karen was saying." Bina wrinkled her brow in concentration. "On the surface, Chimley doesn't seem to have much of a motive. He is rolling in dough."

"Chimley would appreciate that pun," Karen smiled.

Bina chuckled.

"Working for him, I have to endure one pun after another," Karen revealed. "He calls our forks 'threeks' because they have three prongs, not four."

"That's pathetic." Bina rolled her eyes. "Still, even with a lack of obvious motive, it's possible the toothpick in the drawer could link Chimley to the theft. We all know about money's power to corrupt. We've heard of millionaires who were caught embezzling. Maybe he's just money-hungry."

"That doesn't sound like Chimley, but who knows what he's really like?" Karen conceded.

"But Karen, you have my word," Bina

said. "I will not make any accusations until I have uncontestable proof that he did it. If indeed he has."

"Fair enough."

"Okay. Now I have a plan, Karen, but I'll need your help." Bina pushed Mrs. Palanchio's chair back in place. "Can you sleep over at Shira's tonight?"

"I think so. I'll call home and ask."

"Good." Bina slid the phone towards Karen. "We're going to follow the trail of the yucky toothpick."

Chapter Ten

Monday evening, at eight o'clock, an hour after Chimley's closed for the day, the girls were standing in front of his store.

"I'm starting to get edgy." Shira was hopping from one foot to the other. "Go on, Karen. Hurry."

Karen was shaking as she opened the front door to Chimley's and turned on the lights. Bina and Shira waited outside, peering into the bakery's glass window, watching for an all-clear signal from her.

The shelves were empty. Gone were the challahs, breads and cookies. The skeletons of display racks glinted in the light. Only the fake plastic cakes, shaped like baseball diamonds and golf courses, remained in place.

At Shira's house, Thursday night, the three girls had discussed the feasibility of Bina's plan. They agreed not to make any final decisions until after the weekend. Then Sunday evening, sitting on Bina's bed in pajamas, they talked late into the night.

Karen was not happy with Bina's plan. "Sneaking into Chimley's shop and snooping around doesn't seem like the right thing to do."

"Why?" Bina asked. "If he took our money, don't you want to get it back?"

"But it's like biting the hand that feeds me," Karen wailed. "When I needed a job, Chimley gave it to me. He always pays me on time. He is flexible with my hours. He even trusted me with the key to the store. How can I turn on him?"

Bina stuck her toothpick into a cube of melon, the bowl with sliced honeydew, cantaloupe and watermelon on the bed between them.

"Karen, have you ever been to a poker game?"

"No, why?"

"Games take time to play. On baking

night, you were working in the front of the store, so you didn't see what was going on in the back. Shira and I were looking out of the window and we saw those guys who you said came to Chimley's for a poker game. They only stayed a few minutes before zooming out again. Then others came and they did the same thing."

"Really?" Karen was shocked.

"They never stayed long enough to play anything." Bina wiped her chin with a napkin. "Did you ever see a card table or any poker chips lying around?"

"No," Karen said slowly. "No, I've never come across any evidence of a game. Not even a deck of cards."

"Well, then," Bina pressed, "you have to agree that something odd is going on."

"Yeah. But I still don't feel right about it."

They finally agreed on a strategy. Karen would stay in the front of the store doing the bookkeeping while Bina and Shira would snoop around in the back. Since the rear door could only be opened from inside the bakery, Chimley, if he arrived unexpectedly, would enter through the front of the store. That would give the girls time to escape out the back door which, Karen told them, would lock automatically when closed.

"It still doesn't seem right," Karen said morosely.

"Maybe it is bending the rules," Bina agreed, "but what if Chimley is doing something illegal? How would you feel if you had a chance to stop him, but didn't?"

Karen went along with the plan reluctantly. "Okay, but just promise me one thing. Make absolutely certain that this time before you judge the cover, you read the book."

"I'll really try. And I must say," Bina grinned broadly, "that was a lovely metaphor. Mrs. Mitchkin would be very proud of you."

Bina's stomach was churning and she could feel the back of her neck beginning to itch. What if Chimley comes back? What if those men in their sports cars decide to pay a visit tonight?

"If we don't go in soon, I don't think I'll be able to go through with this," Bina whispered.

"You're scared too? Good. I'm glad I'm not the only one who's chicken. Let's call it off. Let's go home, okay? We can get in big trouble. Maybe we can get a loan. Let's tell Karen that she was right and let's get out of here."

Bina grasped her friend's arm. "We can't do that now. We've come this far, we have to continue. Once we get inside, we'll be all right."

Bina was trying to reassure herself more than Shira.

Karen gave the signal and they slowly pushed open the bakery's front door. They nodded to Karen as they ducked under the counter and made their way to the back of the store.

Bina stumbled when her toe caught on a rubber mat. She regained her balance.

"Where are the lights?" Shira whispered.

They did not leave each other's side as they ran their hands along the cold bakery walls.

"Found it." Bina flipped on the switch.

They were in the room where the baking was done. To their surprise, the bakery was immaculate. Everything seemed to be in place. The stainless steel counters and sinks were gleaming, free of the spots that plagued even their fastidious mothers' clean sinks.

"I am impressed," Shira said. With the lights on, they no longer felt the need to whisper. "Chimley never struck me as the neat and clean type. Especially with that grimy jacket he always wears and those yucky toothpicks."

"Perhaps those are just his personal habits. His professional ones seem to be more polished. For the quality bakery goods that he turns out, I guess he would have to be somewhat clean."

"This is all fine and dandy but we didn't come here to perform a spot check on Chimley's baking habits."

Bina chuckled quietly. "I don't feel quite as scared as I did before, but I honestly have no idea what we should look for."

Shira's eyes scanned the room. "Nope,

there's nothing here marked 'clue', nor is there anything that says 'suspicious' in big, bold, black letters." Shira's humor always helped ease tension.

"I guess we should just look for something out of place."

They turned and faced a pile of baking sheets with matching covers.

"Aha!" Shira cried.

"What? A baker is supposed to have baking sheets. It's just one of those things."

"Not a kosher baker." Shira pointed to stickers plastered on the sides of the metal trays.

"Come on," Bina said. "Stickers aren't non-kosher. What's the problem?"

"Don't you remember? We learned that before using new utensils, they have to be immersed in a *mikvah*, a place where they collect rain water in a special way..."

"I remember," Bina cut in. "So?"

"Since the water has to touch every surface of the utensil, or baking sheet in this case, all the stickers have to be removed first."

"There's just one error in your

reasoning," Bina countered. "Chimley isn't Jewish. He doesn't have to dunk his utensils in the *mikvah*. But you may be on to something. Those baking pans have lots of stickers on them but all these others don't have any. These seem out of place."

"Get down, Bina, someone's coming!"

They ducked behind a table.

"It's just me," Karen called as she entered the room. "I just wanted to make sure you weren't knocking anything over or something. Be careful with Chimley's stuff. He still has to make a living, you know."

"Karen, we just found stickers on these baking pans over here," Shira said.

"So what? Where's the law against having stickers? I'll say it once again. You had better be sure you have proof before you open your mouth against Chimley." She spun around and walked out.

"She's not comfortable with the idea that Chimley might be a crook," Bina said, yawning. "She's right though, the baking pans are probably nothing. Let's look in the back room."

Shira turned off the lights in the baking

-125-

area as Bina flicked on the ones in the back room. They inspected this room at a faster pace. At one point, Bina thought she found a hidden drawer, but when she opened it, there were only plastic bags.

Then Shira checked under the loaf racks and her hand struck something smooth. She pulled and twisted until she dislodged a small, worn, gray notebook.

"Bina, look!" Shira blew the flour from the cover, then slowly turned the pages. A few were stuck together. The writing was so faint, both girls had trouble deciphering the scrawled handwriting.

"Three boxes of..." Bina read slowly trying to make out the words. "What does this say?"

"Three boxes of sodium bicarbonate. Hey, do you think Chimley is producing chemical weapons?"

"No, silly. Sodium bicarbonate isn't a foreign chemical. It's baking soda." Bina took the book and flipped through the rest of the pages. "I think we have found a secret here all right, but not the one we are looking for. Looks like we found Chimley's secret cache of recipes. Look, on this page there's the recipe for chocomulas, except here he calls them chocomoles."

"Maybe he changed it because moles wouldn't sell too well," Shira giggled. "Who would want to eat a mole?"

Shira replaced the book as Bina continued looking around the room. Her eyes fell upon a computer perched on a table against the back wall.

"Wow, this is the newest computer on the market. Check it out!" Bina exclaimed. "I've only read about this one in computer magazines."

"It looks like a regular computer to me," Shira wisecracked. "But, then again, I can barely tell the difference between a computer and a typewriter."

"The high-resolution graphics that this computer is capable of producing are supposed to be so advanced that not only can it print out a copy of the Mona Lisa, it can even mimic the brushstrokes and colors." Fascinated, Bina sat down at the keyboard. "And it's amazingly fast when it comes to doing computations."

"I guess Chimley must keep his business records on it," Shira sounded bored, "or his recipes. Maybe he got tired of writing in his little notebook."

"Could be," Bina said thoughtfully, "but he could do that on a regular computer. Why would he need something as state-of-the-art as this?"

Bina looked under the table and picked up a volume explaining the word-processing program. She scanned through the pages. "It doesn't take anything fancy to run this."

"Do you think you're on to something?"

"There's only one way to find out." Bina pressed the power switch. "I'm sure Chimley won't mind me playing with his computer if I promise not to hurt it."

"Be careful, Bina."

"The computer's not going to bite me." Bina's hands danced over the keys. Flashing colors blipped rudely across the screen every few moments. Bina's hands responded with fast typing. Nevertheless, the computer continued its flickering rainbow display.

"It won't let me in." Bina sighed,

disappointed. "It keeps telling me I don't have the correct password. Maybe I could figure it out..."

"Bina, stop!"

Bina eyes didn't move from the computer screen. Shira grabbed her friend's hands. As Bina started to push her away, she clapped a hand over her mouth.

"Chimley's here!" Shira whispered frantically.

"Why didn't you say so?"

"I hope she doesn't give us away," Shira trembled, biting her lower lip so hard that a white streak appeared.

"She won't."

As Shira tiptoed to shut the lights, Bina turned off the computer.

They overheard Karen telling Chimley, "I came in because I wanted to finish this month's bookkeeping records. Sorry if I took you by surprise."

"That's okay, Karen Richy-Rich," Chimley replied cheerfully. "But I'm baking a batch of my chocomulas tonight and since it is a secret recipe, I don't allow anyone to be here while I fix and mix my bag of tricks, ha, ha. You'll understand if I ask you to leave, won't you?"

"No problem." Karen raised her voice, hoping to alert Shira and Bina. "I was getting ready to leave anyway."

"There are delicious chocolate-chip cookies in the freezer. Do you want to take some home?"

By now, Bina and Shira were standing by the open rear door.

"He really is a nice guy," Bina whispered in amazement.

"Yeah, but I don't think he'd be so nice if he found us back here."

Hearing footsteps, Shira pushed Bina out the door and softly closed it behind her. They ran towards the school.

Bina gulped deeply, "That was close."

"Too close."

Karen arrived almost immediately. She did not look very happy.

"Why did you take so long?"

"We had to give the place a thorough search," Shira bristled. "Give us a break. Do you know how scary it was to be there, hearing Chimley out front?"

"It couldn't have been half as scary as confronting my boss and having to lie to him," Karen shot back.

"You were great," Bina praised. "And, I must admit, I view Chimley in a whole new light now. He was really nice about you being there. Charming, even."

"I told you so," Karen said, softening with Bina's words. "Did you find anything?"

"I'm not sure." Bina yawned deeply.

"That's pretty vague." Karen rubbed her eyes. "You look like you're as tired as I am."

"You better believe it. We didn't get very much sleep last night, remember? Is that Chimley's delivery truck?"

"Yes. That truck is another one of Chimley's quirks. During the day, he usually drives a car. But at night, he always drives that truck. I guess he does his deliveries in the evening after the store closes. He has a saleslady for a few hours a day but he said he doesn't like to leave her alone for any length of time." Karen studied the vehicle. "He absolutely loves that truck.

It doesn't look like anything special to me."

"If he loves it so much, why doesn't he drive it during the day also?" Bina asked as they started walking home.

"I dunno. Once he was talking to a customer on the phone and I heard him say, 'Can't fill your order now. Come back tonight when the truck is here.'"

"That's an odd statement," Shira said. "Why would he keep cakes in the truck?"

Karen shrugged. "'Cause he's weird?"

"Was that a poker game night?" Bina yawned again.

"Who remembers."

Chapter Eleven

The dew sparkled on the leaves, evaporating slowly in the early morning sun. The air was cool but held the promise of a beautiful day.

Bina, Shira and Karen had spent another sleepless night together, tracing and retracing past events, thinking and rethinking future directions.

They trudged into school half asleep. They were jolted awake by the scene that greeted them.

Girls were zipping in and out of the classrooms and skipping up and down the halls. Gleeful shouts and laughter were heard above the slamming of locker doors. There was such a festive air, Bina wondered if one of her classmates had gotten engaged.

"Isn't it great?" Estee, waltzing by, grabbed Bina's hand and slapped her five.

Bina stepped back in surprise. "What?"

"You haven't heard? The money's back!"

Bina's mouth fell open.

"Mrs. Palanchio found it this morning in her desk. It was stuck under a pile of papers in the bottom drawer. So we hadn't been robbed after all. Isn't this wonderful?"

Shira and Karen stood speechless.

Bina's thoughts raced furiously. How could the money have been there all along? They had searched everywhere. It wasn't possible! But obviously it was. Having the money back meant no more scary late nights, no more searches, and best of all, it meant that they were going to New York.

Bina's joy bubbled over. She grabbed Shira and Karen and they began to sing and dance around in a circle. Soon the entire twelfth grade joined in. They moved with wild abandon. The nightmare was over. They were going to New York!

Mrs. Schaeffer's approach did not stop the girls' exhilaration. She was pulled into the dancing circle and willingly joined in the festivities.

"Okay girls," Mrs. Schaeffer said breathlessly, after a few minutes. "Time to *daven*. This is definitely a day to express your thanks to *Hashem*."

With reluctance, the twelfth graders broke the circle and wound their way into the auditorium.

After davening, Bina went looking for Karen. Karen had been right to protect Chimley. She was thankful that Karen had restrained her from accusing Chimley outright, and obviously unfairly, since the whole 'robbery' had only been a mix-up.

As Bina approached, she smiled when she saw that she would have to wait in line to talk to Karen. A cluster of girls were swarming around her. They obviously all felt guilty about the way they had treated her. Bina looked at Karen's face. She was beaming, laughing with the girls who had been ignoring her all year.

"Karen, I just want to say that I'm sorry." Goldie chummily clapped her on the back. "It was dumb of me to think that you

-135-

would have done something like that. I guess my mouth got ahead of my brain on that one."

"Don't worry about it, Goldie. I have to ask your forgiveness, too. Remember that time in Mrs. Mitchkin's class? Well, my mouth got ahead of me, too."

"Karen," another voice rang out, "when we get to New York, do you want to..."

Bina was thrilled that everything was working out so well for Karen. *Hashem* works in mysterious ways, she thought. Maybe this whole robbery thing was just to help Karen. Her father has a job now and she is glowing with offers of friendship.

"This is wonderful," Shira murmured, coming to stand beside Bina.

"You read my mind. Who would have believed that it would turn out this way?" Bina turned away from the group. "Didn't you think that Chimley had done it?"

"Of course I did. Why else would I have gone sneaking around in his bakery?"

"It just seems a little odd though, doesn't it. I mean, I'm glad that the money is back and of course I can't wait to go to New

York, but I really thought that I had searched the desk drawer thoroughly."

"That toothpick really had me going. I still wonder how it got there."

"The same way the money did." Bina's voice was solemn. "It was a miracle. All of our prayers and efforts were answered. Maybe it was all just a test to see how we would behave."

"Then I don't think a miracle would have occurred. As soon as the money was stolen, our reactions were terrible. These past few days have been filled with *loshon hora* and nasty rumors."

The bell rang. The girls walked out of the auditorium, in twos and threes, talking animatedly. In the hallway, as they approached Mrs. Mitchkin's classroom, Mrs. Schaeffer motioned to Bina.

"See you later, Shira," Bina said, as she followed the principal into her office.

"I believe this envelope belongs to you." Mrs. Schaeffer smiled, as she handed the found money to Bina. "This has been quite an adventure, hasn't it?"

"It's only just begun."

"My, my, isn't that the truth. To avoid any other possible problems, I would like you to take this money to the bank right now and get a bank check made out to the travel agent."

Bina jauntily dashed out of the school, hugging the envelope tightly to her chest, and skipped into the bank. The story of the found money was so incredible that she quickly told Joan, the teller, and Bill, the security guard, who was standing nearby.

Joan took the bills out of the envelope and counted them. Then she counted them again, concentrating on each bill.

"Excuse me Bina, I'll be right back."

Some minutes went by. Then some more. Bina was getting impatient. She glanced at the wall clock. Mrs. Mitchkin's class would soon be over. When Joan returned, her face looked very grave.

"Bina, there is a problem." Joan's usually smiling face was sad and pained. "All the money you just gave me is counterfeit."

Bina felt as if someone had just punched her in the stomach, hard.

"But how could that be! I got that money from this bank. Don't you remember, Joan? You cashed all the checks for me!"

"I do remember. Please, come into the office and speak with the manager."

As Bina entered the manager's office, she looked into Sally Bentle's deep brown eyes. She saw sympathy and compassion there, and her mood lightened; however, it was short-lived.

"Please, sit down." The desk was crammed with papers. In the center was Bina's forlorn envelope.

"These are not the bills Joan gave you. She gave you uncirculated ones and we keep a record of those serial numbers. I checked on the computer. None of these bills match," the manager said gently. "These are counterfeit and a very poor imitation at that. It seems that someone must have switched the real currency for fakes."

Bina groaned. Intuition had told her that something was amiss when the money had returned so suddenly.

"The bank will give us credit for the money though, right?"

"I'm afraid not. If we were to do that for every customer who walked in with counterfeit bills, we would be out of business."

"But that's not fair," Bina wailed.

"I know," Ms. Bentle said sympathetically. She leaned forward in her chair. "If you went to a diamond merchant with a big piece of glass that had been sold to you as a diamond, do you think he would even consider giving you the diamond's worth for the glass?"

"No...but still...something should be done."

"Lately, we have been seeing more and more of these particular fake bills. Unfortunately, this is the largest amount that has surfaced in one place. The F.B.I. has been trying to find the source."

"How long will that take?"

"I don't know. I'm so sorry, Bina."

She walked back to school in a daze. Bina glared at Chimley's Kosher Chewies as she passed by.

She knocked on Mrs. Schaeffer's door and entered. The principal stopped writing and smiled broadly.

"So when should we go to the travel agent?"

Drained of all energy, Bina sank into a chair and told the principal about the bogus money.

The bell rang.

"Go to class now." Mrs. Schaeffer waved Bina out the door. "I will call the bank manager and then try to reach the detective who's been looking into the theft for me. This is no longer a petty crime. Please don't spread this around just yet, okay?"

Bina nodded sadly.

As the students changed classrooms, Bina pulled Shira aside and told her what happened.

"What are we going to do?" Shira cried.

"All I can think of is that we have to continue looking into Chimley, only this time, like a bug under a microscope."

"Gross, but I think you're right."

"I've been thinking about last night and I just can't help believing that the information we need might be lurking somewhere inside Chimley's computer."

"But you can't get in," Shira pointed out. "You don't know the code."

"Yeah. So we'll have to try to figure it out."

"And how are we going to do that? Obviously, we can't just walk up to Chimley and say 'yo buster, what's the password?'"

"Yes, but if someone would pass by the computer and see what he types in, then that would be a whole other story, now, wouldn't it?"

"Do you think Karen would be willing to do that?" Shira looked doubtful. "You know that she believes he can do no wrong."

"But things have changed since yesterday. This morning everyone was falling all over themselves to beg her forgiveness. I don't think she will want to sacrifice her new-found acceptance for Chimley."

At lunchtime, Bina and Shira went looking for Karen. They pried her away from a group of girls and out of the lunchroom. Bina was right. Karen did not need much convincing to continue the investigation. They acquiesced to the principal's request not to tell anyone yet.

After school let out that day, twelve girls from Miami High went home planning their wardrobes for New York. Three girls, Bina, Shira and Karen, had other plans on their mind.

Bina and Shira waited tensely by the telephone in the Gold residence. Every time the phone rang, they both jumped. Even Mrs. Gold's fudge cookies did not soothe their nerves. Karen had gone to work. She would call if she heard or saw anything suspicious going on at Chimley's or, if, by some miracle, she chanced upon his password.

"Bina, do you think Chimley is the counterfeiter?"

"I'm trying not to jump to conclusions but it seems to me that somehow he's connected with all this in some way."

"Why do you think that?"

"I just feel in my gut that he took the money. And if that's true, it stands to reason that he put it back. Then that would make the counterfeit money his, wouldn't it?"

"Maybe he didn't know it was counterfeit." Shira tried giving Chimley the benefit of the doubt. "Don't forget, we don't have any proof."

The phone rang. Bina grabbed it.

"Hi, it's me."

"Karen!" Each girl pressed an ear to the receiver.

"I have to talk fast. Chimley will be back in a few minutes. The strangest thing just happened. I was working at the front counter and a customer came in."

"Now that is very strange," Shira said dryly.

"He was kind of wandering around the bakery and pretending to be interested in the cookies. I finally asked, 'Can I help you?' and he lowered his sunglasses..."

"Sunglasses!" Bina interrupted. "Was he one of the poker players?"

"I...I think so. I've seen him here before. Chimley always waits on him, but he hadn't come back yet. So, the guy leans over the counter and motions for me to come closer."

"I can't stand the suspense," Shira murmured.

"He asks me, 'how much are the chocomulas going for today?'"

"So what?" Bina was puzzled. "Why is that so unusual? You are the salesperson."

"Chimley was just coming in the front door and heard his question. He went absolutely berserk, raving mad, screaming at the guy. I never saw him so angry. 'Why are you asking her about chocomulas? She knows nothing about the chocomulas. You have no brains in that stupid head of yours, asking a question like that of her. Get out of here! I don't serve dumb people.'"

"Then what happened?" Bina asked breathlessly.

"The guy ran out of the store and Chimley calmed down a little. He apologized and mumbled something about being under a lot of pressure and...gotta go, Chimley's back..." Click. The phone went dead.

Bina sat numbly with the receiver in her

hand. "We have to go back there...we have to go back to Chimley's, tonight."

Chapter Twelve

At eight o'clock that evening, Bina and Shira crept silently to the front of Chimley's Kosher Chewies. Seeing Karen standing behind the counter, they breathed sighs of relief.

Earlier, they had agreed that Karen would give Chimley some excuse that would allow her to be in the bakery that night. But until they saw Karen there they weren't sure if she would actually go through with it.

They knocked softly.

"What did you tell him?" Bina asked, as Karen unlocked the door.

"That I had a test and needed a quiet place to study. Chimley had no problem letting me study here."

"Good." She ducked under the counter.

"If you hear anything, call out 'challah'. That way Shira and I will know that we have to get out fast."

"I'll do my best."

Karen switched on the lights in the baking area and waited until Bina and Shira entered the back room. She then turned them off and returned to the front of the store.

"Shira, as soon as I get the computer up and running, turn off the lights, okay?"

"Isn't it bad for your eyes to work in the dark?"

"Yes, but it will be a lot worse for more than my eyes if we get caught."

They both gulped down the fright creeping over them. An impromptu prayer for success escaped Bina's lips as she made her way to the computer.

As the mighty machine whirred to life, she immediately began tapping the keys, going through the preliminary mazes of computer protocol. Then the screen went blank except for the blinking cursor. Time for the password.

"Have you figured out the code?" Shira

asked nervously, peering over her shoulder in the dark.

"Maybe," Bina said and pronounced aloud each letter that she typed, "C-H-O-C-O-M-U-L-A."

The computer rejected it. Bina's hands slammed down on the keyboard.

She turned her head trying to ignore the riotous colors flashing across the screen with the word 'Error'.

"I was so sure that was it because Chimley got so angry when the guy asked Karen about the chocomulas."

"It did sound right," Shira comforted her...then exploded, "Wait! Remember that recipe book I found? Maybe he uses that other spelling of chocomulas."

Bina sprang to life.

C-H-O-C-O-M-O-L-E, she typed.

The computer began humming happily and proceeded to the next screen.

"You're brilliant, Shira!"

"We did it," Shira squealed.

"Not so fast. We still don't know what we're looking for."

"Challah! Challah! Challah!" Karen

yelled.

Bina and Shira froze.

Karen came running in. "Chimley just called and said that he'll be here in five or ten minutes. He said he needs stuff from the freezer to make some deliveries."

"Don't panic," a panicky Bina said to herself. "I just have to work faster."

"Karen, that was a great practice run of the challah alert system." Shira attempted humor in a humorless situation. "Now go back and do it again when you see him arriving."

Karen turned and fled.

Bina hunched over the computer. The titles of each different program were displayed in a separate square on the screen. There were bakery files, recipe files and accounting files.

"Nothing out of the ordinary here," Bina mumbled.

Rapidly pointing and clicking the mouse device attached to the computer's side, she reduced the size of each square.

"Bingo," Bina whispered as the last box scaled down.

Behind the square was a whole new set of boxes containing more program files.

"Art. Chocomula Orders. Supplies. Directions," Bina read. "Let's see Chocomula Orders."

A neat table sprang up on the screen. It listed names, addresses, quantities and account balances.

"Maybe these are Chimley's special chocomula customers," Bina exhaled. "I'm going to print this. Grab everything that comes out of the printer, okay?"

Shira nodded, her face pale and her hands shaking.

The printer spilled out the copies at high speed.

"He uses such bright-colored paper," Shira mumbled, as she snatched the pages.

"What could Directions be? Let's check it out, okay?"

"Whatever you say, Bina. Just hurry."

"Hang in there, Shira."

"I wish I was there and not here."

"Stay cool. Soon we won't be here."

When Bina scanned the contents of the directions file, she was confused. Instead of file names, there were just dates. They spanned many days and weeks. She did not know which one to pick. Then she saw today's date. She triggered the print command.

"Challah, challah, challah," Karen shouted.

A moment later, they heard Chimley's voice as the front door opened. "Is that my number-crunchin' Karen?"

"Yeah, hi. I don't feel so good. I was just going to go home."

Bina and Shira waited impatiently for the printer to spit out the document. Seconds seemed like hours, as they stood with bated breath, praying for the last page to slide out quickly.

Shira opened the door as the printer gave birth to the final sheet. Bina grabbed the page and flicked off the computer switch. Just as Chimley turned on the light in the baking area, the back door softly clicked shut.

"We're okay. We're okay." Shira was breathing quickly as she handed the pages to Bina. "I thought we were going to be caught for sure."

"Me too," Bina folded the papers. "Look, there's Chimley's delivery truck and the back door is open. Let's take a peek inside. I'm curious to see what's so special about that truck."

"But Chimley might come out any minute!"

"Nah, he just got here." Bina put the computer printouts in her pocket. "He has to put together the delivery orders first."

Her words reassured Shira and they ran to the truck, parked near the back fence, close to the bushes.

Shira climbed up the step and stood in the doorway facing the lit interior.

"Wow, it's neat in here," she said. "It reminds me of a house trailer with separate areas."

"Let's go through it quickly," Bina said. "Take note of anything unusual."

Bina put a foot on the metal step as Shira moved inside. From the corner of her eye, she noticed the bakery's rear door opening.

"Chimley's coming," she breathed softly, "get out."

She dove behind a nearby bush, just as Chimley exited the bakery. Shira did not follow her.

To Bina's horror, Chimley crossed straight to the truck. Had Shira heard her warning? Was she aware that Chimley was there?

"Please, *Hashem*, don't let her make a sound," Bina prayed fervently.

Chimley reached up and pulled down the sliding door. It slithered down like a serpentine window blind and closed with a hiss.

Shira was trapped inside!

Chapter Thirteen

Bina stood frozen in the darkness, the only bright light coming from the bakery's interior, through the open back door. She had no idea what to do. She jumped when she felt something press against her arm. It was Karen.

"Shira's locked inside the truck," she stammered into Karen's ear.

"I know. I saw what happened. Maybe Chimley will go back into the bakery."

She could barely hear Karen's words. She took her hand and held it tightly.

"Oh no, look!" Karen pointed.

A line of headlights were heading into the alley.

"I thought Chimley said he had to make some deliveries. Is he having one of his

-155-

'poker games' tonight?"

Karen missed the sarcasm in Bina's voice. "Looks like it, doesn't it? And those games can go on forever. I just don't understand anything anymore."

"It's not the length of time that worries me. I would wait here all night if it meant getting Shira out safely. But I'm beginning to think that Chimley's deliveries and his poker games are somehow connected. I'm beginning to think that maybe it's not poker he's playing, but some game that's very dangerous."

A crazed pattern of lights and shadows fell across Chimley's face as he stood in the path of the oncoming cars. Bina and Karen held their breaths as Chimley side-stepped towards them.

"Welcome, my friends. Welcome," Chimley said loudly and nodded to each of the occupants in the Porsches, Ferraris and Lamborghinis. "Who is here for the chocomulas?"

As the word chocomulas was spoken, the men got out of their cars. Bina was not surprised to see each one wearing sunglasses in the dark of the night.

Chimley retreated into the bakery. One by one, the men went inside for about half a minute. Each emerged with a covered baking tray and drove off.

"Those are the trays Shira spotted in the bakery last night," Bina said, noticing the white labels. "We thought they looked out of place."

They watched one man, standing in the glare of his headlights, his car parked near the girls' hiding place, lift the tray's cover. A bright orange paper fluttered to the ground. Bina caught a glimpse of lines and drawings. A map, perhaps? The man retrieved the paper, darted into his car and departed.

"Why are these men coming here for pieces of paper?" Bina whispered.

"Forget the questions. We have to find a way to get Shira out of the truck."

"Do you notice that every few minutes, more cars arrive? It seems unending."

"They're going to have to stop sometime," Karen replied tersely.

"Poor Shira, I hope she's okay in there."

"If it's filled with bakery goods, she will be. Although I'd guess that after this, she'll never again want to touch another cookie."

"Hey, I have a plan."

"I don't want to hear it," Karen choked. "That's how Shira got stuck in the truck in the first place."

"Please, listen to me."

"Okay, what?" Karen could not keep the nervousness out of her voice.

"It's simple. All you have to do is distract Chimley."

"If it's so simple, why don't you do it?"

"Because, Karen, I have no business being at Chimley's so late at night."

"And I do?"

"Can't you just say that you forgot one of your books at the bakery?"

Karen thought a moment. "That doesn't sound too bad."

"There seems to be a pattern to these comings and goings. As a group of cars arrive, Chimley mentions chocomulas and they go inside then, one by one, they emerge with a tray and leave. A few minutes later, Chimley is back at the door, waiting for the next bunch and the whole process is repeated." Bina twirled a strand of hair nervously. "So here's my idea. When the last of a group of cars leaves, run around the school building to the front and go into Chimley's. Distract him. Make some kind of conversation to stop him from going back immediately to the rear door."

"Okay, I'll try it. I'm really afraid for Shira's safety."

"Good luck."

Bina estimated that it would take Karen forty seconds to get around to the front of Miami High. Plus another sixty seconds, hopefully more, talking to Chimley. Then about ten to fifteen seconds before more chocomula 'customers' would arrive.

She counted off forty seconds after Karen left, and waited an extra five to make sure that she reached the front of the bakery. Then she ran to the delivery truck.

She was immediately blinded by headlights from oncoming cars. She jumped to the side of the truck facing away from the bakery. Precious time was being lost.

Suddenly, she heard heavy footsteps

running. A car door opened and closed. Unexpectedly, the truck's red brake lights came on as simultaneously the engine thundered abruptly and the truck roared out of the parking lot.

Bina was too late. She started running after it, no longer caring whether or not the men in the sports cars could see her. All she could think of was poor Shira locked in a truck, being whisked away by bad people, and that it was all her fault.

The delivery truck tilted precariously as it cut a sharp right out of the alley. The sports cars followed.

"Karen," Bina shouted. "Karen, where are you?"

"I'm here." Karen was running up the alley. "By the time I got inside, Chimley was gone. What should we do?"

"Is your bike here?"

"Yes."

"C'mon, quick."

"You don't think we can catch up with the truck, do you?"

"No, we just have to see which way they're going."

"Okay, you wait here."

"Hurry."

Karen pedaled away quickly.

Bina felt lost and alone and terrified. She thought of Shira and shuddered. Then she did what Jewish people have done throughout the ages in times of despair. She said a chapter of *Tehillim*, Psalms.

She walked to the front of the school and sat down on a cement ledge. In the glare of a street light, she took out the computer printouts and began to study them The papers were a bright orange color. On one page there was a map with many lines drawn on it. It looked like a copy of the one the man dropped in the parking area, but she couldn't be sure. She puzzled over it, trying to figure out what it meant.

By the time Karen returned, Bina had a plan.

"Which way did they go?" Bina asked before the bike came to a standstill.

"Luckily they got stuck at a few red lights, although for some they didn't stop at all." She was panting heavily. "So I was able to keep them in sight. They took the highway, heading east."

"Let me ride now. You can hardly breathe."

"Where are we going?"

"To your house."

"My house? How's that going to help Shira?"

Bina mounted the bike and Karen jumped on the back. "I can't ride fast and talk at the same time. I'll explain it all when we get there. We're going after Shira."

Chapter Fourteen

"I think we should call the police," Karen said, as they ran up her front steps.

"And what would we tell them? Our friend was kidnapped? But she wasn't. Chimley's a crook? Where's the proof. They are all...where? We don't know. The police will just think we're a couple of kooks."

"So, what do you suggest we do?" Karen groaned as she faced Bina on the top step. "What can we do?"

"Look, I have an idea. Is your mother or father home?"

"No, they're both working late. Why?"

"Oh, no," Bina's hand flew to her mouth. "I should have asked you that before we came here. My parents are out tonight but I sort of assumed one of yours would be home." She kicked at a pebble on the step. "You see, we need someone who can drive, and drive fast."

"Why?"

"I was studying these printouts from Chimley's computer while you were gone." She pulled out the pages. "This is a map, see? It looks like the paper that man dropped earlier. There is an x mark here, east of where we are. I thought maybe they went there." Bina looked mournfully at Karen. "It's the only thing I can come up with."

Without a word, Karen turned, unlocked the door and ran down the hall to her room. Bina followed, remembering the last time she had been there—to determine if Karen had taken the money. How quickly things change, she thought. Karen, once a suspect, is now my partner.

Karen flung open her bedroom door. "You remember my sister, Sara? She just got her driver's license," Karen said breathlessly. "After failing three times, she finally passed the test."

"How nice of you to let everyone know," drawled the teenager, whose stringbean legs were draped over the bed's footboard. "Next you'll want to show off my ugly license picture. When are you going to stop teasing me, Karen?"

"I'm not teasing you, Sara, it's just that we're in trouble and we desperately need your help."

"You see, our friend is trapped in a truck with dangerous men," Bina cut in. "We need you to drive us so we can find her."

"A rescue mission, huh? Well I'm busy. It's after ten o'clock and I have tons of homework. I'm afraid you'll have to find someone else. I mean, after all, I did fail the test a couple of times." Sara threw back her curly head and laughed. "For sure you wouldn't want me to do the driving."

"Sara, this is not a joke," Karen shouted. "For once in your life, can't you just do something for me? We need your help, and we need it now!"

Sara had obviously received all the easy-going genes in the family. Sara, calm and jolly, was uptight Karen's exact opposite.

"Sara, we need you to drive." Bina said softly, trying the positive approach. "Just think, it will be like an adventure and it will, for sure, break up a boring, daily routine. And anyway, saving a person's life, *pikuach nefesh*, comes before any other commandment," Bina grinned wickedly, "and homework isn't even a commandment."

Bina's right, Sara thought. This could be fun.

"Okay," Sara jumped up. "You're absolutely right, homework can wait. Tell Micha to babysit, Karen, and I'll get the car keys."

As they were leaving, Karen thrust a phone into Bina's hand and grabbed her brother Micha's walkie-talkies from the table.

"My brother said I could take these and I'll feel safer having my Dad's cell phone with us."

"Do you have a flashlight?" Bina asked.

"There's one in the glove compartment," Sara answered.

The family's gray, dented sedan was

parked in the driveway. Sara hesitantly slid behind the wheel, sinking into the stained, worn upholstery. She tentatively adjusted the mirrors and readjusted them with uncertainty.

"This is the first time I'll be driving at night. Are you sure you want me to drive?"

"Sara, stop wasting time!" Karen commanded from the back seat. "If we don't hurry, who knows what will happen to Shira."

"Well, here goes nothing." Sara started the motor. "Hey, it works! Okay, where to?"

"Do you know how to get to the highway?" Bina was sitting in the passenger's seat, going over Chimley's map.

"No."

"Great."

"I know the way," Karen said. "When I was tailing Chimley's truck, he drove down Arthur Godfrey Boulevard, then turned down another street. I don't know its name, but I can direct you."

With Karen's precise directions and Sara's haphazard navigation, the Richter mobile was soon bumping down the highway, heading east.

The car weaved as Sara tried to stay in her lane. She was twisting the steering wheel back and forth like a pendulum. Bina was getting dizzy.

"I think if you just hold the steering wheel lightly without moving it, the car will go straight," Bina volunteered helpfully.

"Talk about a back seat driver," Sara drawled, smiling.

Bina filled her in on the missing money and Chimley's suspect activities, how they found the toothpick, the advanced computer and the fake poker games.

"Do you know where we are going?" Sara asked, not taking her eyes off the road. "Try to tell me early on so I can change lanes in advance."

"Stay in the right lane. It's the next exit."

Bina checked the map again as the car exited the highway.

"Make a right on Jeffress Way and then a left on Wendela Street."

After a few blocks, Karen shouted, "You

just passed Jeffress Way. You're not looking where you're going! Do you think you're driving by radar?"

"Karen, I can't drive and look at street signs at the same time," Sara said patiently. "You have to watch for the signs and tell me when to turn. However, I can easily get back to Jeffress Way. No problemo." She slammed on the brakes and turned the steering wheel sharply to the left. The car careened around in a surprisingly graceful U-turn. "Not bad, huh?"

After a few more wrong turns, Sara finally turned into the last street marked on Chimley's map. She maneuvered the car slowly along the bleak, semi-lit road which was flanked by row after row of warehouses.

"Do you think we are in the right place?" she asked. "Or did I make another wrong turn?"

"I don't know. I thought this was right." Bina eyes returned to the map. "But maybe we did make a wrong turn somewhere. Or maybe I'm completely wrong. Maybe this map has nothing at all to do with where they went." She looked out the window. "I don't see any sign of Chimley or his sports car friends."

Unexpectedly, their car was illuminated by headlights from behind.

"Someone wants to pass you, Sara. Pull over and let them go by."

A low-slung, red Porsche passed them and a few feet ahead, made a sharp right turn onto a dirt driveway with thick bushes and trees on both sides.

"That sure looks like Chimley's type of chocomula customer," Bina said excitedly. "Sara, turn off your headlights and pull the car off the road. Park between those trees."

"Are you nuts?"

"If they are close by, we don't want to be spotted," Karen said sharply.

Sara shrugged, turned off the lights and drove into the dirt area. She slammed on the brakes, almost hitting the bushes.

"Now what?" she asked, turning off the ignition. "I hope you don't expect me to go rescue your friend. I'm not even getting out of this car. I'm just plain chicken."

"Look, I'm scared too," Bina acknowledged. "Maybe Karen was right. Maybe we should call the police."

"I second that," Sara responded immediately.

"Okay, let's do this." Bina's voice was shaking. "Karen and I are going to see if Chimley is here. If he's not, we'll be back in a jiffy. But if he is, we'll beep you on the walkie-talkie. Then, as soon as you hear the beep, call the police." She handed Sara the phone. "Make up something real scary. Tell them there are guys with guns and that they kidnapped your friend. Tell them anything, just make it sound so dangerous, that they'll come fast. And tell them exactly where we are. Here's the map and the flashlight."

She dumped everything in Sara's lap and in no time, the two girls were inching their way up the dirt path through the bushes.

Abruptly, Bina put her hand in front of Karen. "There's Chimley's truck."

Peering out from behind a thick bush, they had a good view of the large dirt area in front of a warehouse. Chimley's truck was surrounded by a number of fancy cars.

From the warehouse roof, two spotlights, insufficient lighting for such a large area, cast eerie shadows around the vehicles. Two men were standing near the back of the truck.

"I don't think they have discovered Shira yet," Karen said cautiously. "The back of the truck is still closed."

"Let's get closer so we can hear what they're saying."

Karen quickly beeped Sara, then followed Bina. Moving stealthily forward, from bush to bush, Bina's stocking caught on a branch. Pulling her foot free, she felt it tear.

The two men were arguing. One was Chimley.

"I told you I have the money," Chimley was shouting. "It's in the truck. Let me get it."

"Chimley, I've heard all this so many times before, that it's become a joke. You always say the same things and you always lie. Your words and promises mean nothing."

"Why'd you call and tell me to get here real fast? Where's the emergency?"

"Here's the emergency." He pointed a gun at Chimley's head. "I can't take care of such business on city streets."

The girls nearly fainted.

"I'm telling you the truth, Felix. This time, I really have the money I owe you. Real money."

"Yeah, right. You just want to go inside your truck to get your gun," Felix snarled menacingly. "You think I'm stupid? I don't have to take any more of your excuses and I don't want that garbage from your truck."

"Garbage? My new computer produced an almost perfect design for the printing press plates..."

"You call that almost perfect?" Felix sneered. "The computer might be capable of creating a near-perfect design, but you sure don't know how. The glaring mistakes on your bills hits ya' like a ton of bricks." He lowered his hand holding the gun. "The money you make is so bogus, it melts in my wallet. How dare you attempt to pay me with worthless paper. Who do you think you are?"

"I'll never do that again, Felix. I swear. I'm so sorry," Chimley whimpered. "Please don't hurt me. We need each other. I'm a good source of income for you and you know how much I need you." Chimley ran his fingers through his hair. "Without the paper you supply, I wouldn't be able to do anything. And who would distribute my counterfeit money?"

His finger jerked nervously at his collar. "And you were absolutely right, the bakery truck is a good cover for the printing press. I follow all of your instructions. I use the school's phone to call you so the calls can't be traced to me. You know you can always count on me."

He took a toothpick from his pocket and started chomping on it. "And you have to admit," he said lightly, trying to diffuse the other man's anger, "that the maps I print, so the men know where to meet you after each pickup, are clear, colorful and accurate—a real work of art."

"Who cares about the maps, Chimley. I wish your money was a work of art. But I want my money now." Felix again pointed the gun at Chimley.

"Have the girls next door left any more money for you?"

"Did you hear that?" Bina whispered indignantly. "Chimley really did steal our money!"

"I can't believe what I'm hearing," Karen moaned softly. "How could he..."

"Karen, let's focus on Shira. What can we do to get her out of the truck?"

"We might be too late." Karen gestured towards the men. Felix and Chimley turned towards the back of the truck. "I think they're about to open the door."

Bina grabbed the walkie talkie and hit the "talk" button.

"Sara, did you call the police?"

"Yes, I hope they believed me."

"Look, you have to drive over here fast. We need to stall for time and divert Chimley's attention away from the truck. He's about to open the back door."

"Are you kidding? What would I do?"

"I don't know. Anything. Just distract them anyway you can. Use your acting ability, but hurry."

A minute later, Sara rattled up the drive, her old banged-up car a sore thumb alongside the expensive, shiny vehicles. All eyes watched as the car jerked to a halt and Sara waltzed out. Her hair was out of its ponytail, her curls swinging around her shoulders.

"Oh, thank heaven y'all are here," she drawled in a high falsetto. "Ah am so lost. Ah just can't find my way. Ah must get to the highway. Ah'm on my way to Georgia. It's my weddin' day tomorrow and ah mustn't be late. Everyone would think ah just ran off and left Billy Joe standin' at the altar."

Bina and Karen bit their lips to keep from laughing out loud.

"Excuse me, sir. Excuse me," Sara sang, waving her hands wildly, approaching the two men near the truck.

"Get her out of here," Chimley snarled. "Someone get rid of her before I get really angry." No one moved. Chimley turned and glared at Sara. "Get out of here, you hear? Get out now! I will count to ten and if you aren't out of here..."

"Yo, Jacko, take it easy," a man called from one of the cars. "This young lady just wants directions. She ain't after your chocomulas, man. Be nice and give her one of your maps."

Chimley whipped out an orange paper from his pocket and thrust it as Sara. Felix showed her the way to the highway on the map. Sara made a full curtsy, then slowly returned to her car and drove off.

Chimley immediately spun around and slid up the truck's metal door. The interior lights came on automatically.

Bina inhaled sharply. She craned her neck but could not see Shira. Blocking her view was a wall of boxes in the center, which Bina assumed held fake bills, not chocomulas.

Chimley climbed into the truck, disappeared for a moment, then returned, handing a wad of bills to Felix. As Felix counted the money, each sports car rolled in closer. He nodded, satisfied, and handed the money through the window of one of the cars.

"Due to the 'emergency' interruption of

your chocomula distribution, Chimley, these guys," Felix waved towards the cars, "didn't get their share yet. Are those boxes ready to go?"

"After the bills are printed, I always put them into the store's freezer. Cold cash, y'know. Ha, ha," Chimley guffawed. "But these guys are lucky. They get dough hot from the oven." He threw his head back and laughed heartily.

He started handing down boxes to Felix who, in turn, passed them through each window. Little by little, the wall of boxes, and, Bina assumed, Shira's wall of protection, was coming down.

Extreme fear and tension exploded in Bina. She lost it. She dashed out from her hiding place, screaming.

Felix whipped out his gun. Chimley, recognizing Bina, yelled, "Hey, what are you doing here?"

Bina stood there sobbing hysterically. She closed her eyes and began begging *Hashem* for mercy.

Suddenly, a loud, gruff voice bellowed, "POLICE! FREEZE! Throw your guns down!" Guns thumped onto the dirt. "Now get out of your cars slowly with your hands in the air!"

Muttering curses, the men did as they were told and soon all were in custody.

In the commotion, Bina scrambled up into the truck. Her eyes never saw the printing press or the piles of fresh twenty-dollar bills on top of it. She saw only Shira, curled up on the floor in the back of the truck.

"Are you okay?" Bina fell to her knees and hugged her tightly, both girls shaking fiercely.

"I was so scared," Shira sobbed.

"I know. I know." Bina was crying too, as they rocked each other back and forth. "But do you realize we solved the mystery of the missing money?" She took a wad of tissues out of her pocket and handed one to Shira. "And without you, we would never have had proof of Chimley's guilt." She smiled, wiping away her tears. "And a bonus was you found his counterfeiting machine."

"That's really great, Bina," her voice still

shaking with sobs, "but I just want to go home and never ever leave it again. It's too dangerous out here in the real world."

"What? You don't even want to go to New York?" Bina teased.

Shira smiled weakly. "Well maybe, but promise me something."

"Anything."

"Promise to carry my wallet for me in New York. I don't ever want to be this close to money again."

Chapter Fifteen

The first call came from Karen's mother. Mrs. Gold grabbed the phone, hoping it was Bina. She listened as the almost hysterical parent related that Bina, Karen and Sara had left their house hours ago, taking the family car, without permission, and had not returned.

"...and Sara such a new and inexperienced driver."

Bina's mother suggested that they come to the Gold's house and decide together what to do. As soon as she hung up, the phone rang again. It was Shira's mom wanting to know if the girls were there.

"Shira left a note saying she was going to meet Bina at school and that she would not be back late," the distraught voice trembled.

"It's almost midnight and she's not home yet."

Mrs. Gold told her about the Richter's phone call and asked that they come over too. Each of the girls' parents had been out that evening and when they had returned home after 10:30 p.m., their children were not there.

Rabbi Gold drove to the school, only to find it dark and locked. Upon returning home, he called the principal, wanting to know if any activity had been scheduled at school that evening. Mrs. Schaeffer said no and after hearing about the missing girls, asked that they call her as soon as they heard any news.

The three sets of parents now sat in the Gold's living room and all agreed that the police should be called. As Rabbi Gold went to the phone, it rang.

"Bina! Where are you?" He paused a moment, listening. "What happened...?"

Everyone crowded around him.

"Okay, honey, take it easy. Everything will be okay," he said soothingly. "Shira's and Karen's parents are here, so come straight home. Tell Sara to drive slowly and carefully. And try to calm down, sweetheart. See you soon."

As he hung up, everyone began asking questions at once.

"Wait, please." He raised his hands. "I'll tell you what she said but it's not much. She wouldn't say anything except that they would explain everything when they got home. She sounded all shaken up but, *Boruch Hashem*, thank G-d, the girls are safe and on their way home." He turned back to the phone. "I must call Mrs. Schaeffer. She is anxiously waiting to hear good news."

Upon hearing that the girls were okay, Mrs. Schaeffer said, "I was just on my way to your house. I'll be there shortly." When she arrived, she joined the parents in their tense vigil.

After what seemed like an eternity, the chug-a-lug of the old car was heard pulling into the driveway and they ran to the door. Their daughters threw themselves into their mothers' outstretched arms, holding on very tightly.

As everyone was settling down in the living room, Mrs. Gold went into the kitchen and returned with a tray of cookies and hot cocoa for the girls.

"I'm sure you girls realize how worried we have been tonight," Rabbi Gold began, "but we will reserve any judgment until after we have heard your explanations." He looked at each of the four girls. "Who will start?"

Their words tumbled out, each interrupting the other, until slowly the story was pieced together.

"We would have called sooner," Bina added, when the shaken and exhausted girls finished their story, "but the police spent a lot of time questioning us. They said the money Chimley had given Felix tonight was more than enough to repay our stolen money."

"Chimley," Karen's mother said slowly. "Who would have ever suspected Chimley."

"But he would never have hurt us," Karen said glumly. "Those other thugs probably would have, but not Chimley."

Bina and Shira exchanged glances. After

all that had happened, Karen was still defending Chimley.

The next day, the girls came late to school. Reporters and photographers were waiting for them outside the building. As they began to tell their stories and pose for pictures, students and teachers, Mrs. Schaeffer and even Mrs. Palanchio hurried out of Miami High, and crowded around trying to catch every word.

When they finished, a loud cheer erupted and the students began clapping. Mrs. Schaeffer asked everyone to return to class. In the hallway, all the girls wanted to hear the details again and again.

"What did chocomulas have to do with everything?" Estee asked.

"Chocomulas were not real pastries," Bina explained. "Chimley used it as a password with the hoodlums."

"No, Bina, chocomulas are real cakes," Karen said pensively, "but I never heard anyone order any. Once in a while, Chimley did make some, but no one ever bought them. He always ended up giving them away as presents, maybe to celebrate real good counterfeiting days." Karen rolled her eyes. "He even gave me one once," she grinned. "It was out of this world."

Everyone laughed.

Then Karen's smile turned into a frown. "He was always making those terrible puns. Had I paid closer attention, maybe I would have realized that chocomulas was another one of his sick jokes...mula or moola being slang for money."

"Didn't you or any of the bakers working there find it weird to see dollar bills lying around the store?" Goldie asked.

"He didn't leave them around. Turns out he kept them in the locked freezer. Cold cash, Chimley called it."

Leah giggled.

"And there were no other bakers, just Chimley," Karen looked at Bina, "who it turns out, didn't do much baking."

"What? How could that be? His shelves were always overflowing with goodies."

"My father questioned the *mashgiach* early this morning," Bina said. "It seems Chimley bought most everything from the

Shomer Shabbos bakery across town."

Cries of disbelief echoed through the hall.

"He did do some baking," Karen said, almost defensively, "but not much."

"He kept this a secret because he was afraid he would lose customers who would think the items weren't fresh," Shira explained.

"The *mashgiach* knew about the arrangement but said his job was only to make sure everything in the store was kosher," Bina said, "which it was."

"No wonder the baking area was so immaculate," Shira grimaced.

"Hey, guess what," Rena said elatedly. "Now we can use all the money from the bake sale to help the needy."

Karen nodded enthusiastically, knowing that her parents were now able to pay for her trip.

As they entered the classroom, Mrs. Mitchkin was standing near her desk, smiling. She waited until everyone was seated before speaking.

"On behalf of everyone here, I want to

thank you girls for salvaging our trip to the Big Apple," and with a theatrical display, she withdrew three shiny red apples and presented them to Bina, Shira and Karen. Everyone applauded loudly. "I still can't believe that it was Jacko Chimley. He seemed so pleasant."

"A lot of us didn't turn out to be what we seemed to be," Bina said sadly, looking at her classmates. "Remember when poor Mrs. Palanchio was a suspect?"

Everyone groaned.

"And then me," Karen spoke quietly. "It's a terrible thing to be judged before all the facts are known. Take it from one who knows."

"I believe you have all learned a tremendous lesson from this unfortunate incident." Mrs. Mitchkin looked gravely at each student. "Not judging a book by its cover, being *'dan l'kaf zechus'*, giving someone the benefit of the doubt, is an important *midah*, a quality that all of us have to work on strenuously. It's not easy to look at someone and completely avoid forming some kind of opinion, but, perhaps now, you can see the importance of reserving judgment before all the facts are known. Just think of how much hurt would have been avoided if we had given people the benefit of the doubt and didn't speak maliciously about them." Mrs. Mitchkin paused, watching her students absorbing her words.

"And now, I have a surprise for all of you. Late last night, when Mrs. Schaeffer called to tell me what had happened, I knew that today would be a day to celebrate. I'll be back in a moment."

As the teacher left the room, Rena asked, "Did your parents punish you?"

"Yeah," the three girls said simultaneously.

"But it's not too steep," Bina said, "because we didn't do it behind their backs or anything. They just weren't home for us to ask them for help and we couldn't wait. We had to save Shira."

"We got punished mainly for not telling them beforehand about our plans to snoop around Chimley's store at night," Karen said.

"And for not being truthful about why we went to school that evening when we were looking for clues," Shira added.

Mrs. Mitchkin returned back with a bakery box filled to the brim with pastries. "And, I assure you, these are not from Chimley's Chewies." Everyone burst out laughing. "Help yourselves, girls, and enjoy."

In bed that evening, Bina's mind kept retracing all the events of the past few days. Snooping around school and at Chimley's hadn't seemed dangerous...it was such familiar territory. But taking off after the counterfeiters was indeed dangerous. At the time, however, all she could think of was Shira's safety. She shuddered at the thought that the ordeal could have had a tragic ending instead of a happy one.

After all the twists and turns of this unbelievable experience, it is a miracle that the trip will actually take place. Her sleepy thoughts drifted from counterfeiters to skyscrapers and she fell asleep dreaming of the Bais Yaakov Convention and of all the exciting things to do and see in New York City.